A FACE LIKE THE MOON

A FACE LIKE THE MOON

MINA ATHANASSIOUS

Library and Archives Canada Cataloguing in Publication

Athanassious, Mina, 1987-, author
    A face like the moon : stories / Mina Athanassious.

Issued in print and electronic formats.
ISBN 978-1-77161-339-2 (softcover).--ISBN 978-1-77161-340-8 (HTML).--ISBN 978-1-77161-341-5 (Kindle)

    I. Title.

PS8601.T49F33 2018   C813'.6   C2018-902073-3
                                                                                          C2018-902074-1

No part of this book may be reproduced or transmitted in any form, by any means, electronic or mechanical, including photocopying and recording, information storage and retrieval systems, without permission in writing from the publisher, except by a reviewer who may quote a brief passage in a review.

Published by Mosaic Press, Oakville, Ontario, Canada, 2018.
MOSAIC PRESS, Publisher

Copyright © 2018 Mina Athanassious
Design by Courtney Blok
Printed and Bound in Canada

ONTARIO ARTS COUNCIL
CONSEIL DES ARTS DE L'ONTARIO
an Ontario government agency
un organisme du gouvernement de l'Ontario

We acknowledge the Ontario Arts Council
for their support of our publishing program

We acknowledge the Ontario Media Development Corporation
for their support of our publishing program

Funded by the   Financé par le
Government   gouvernement | Canadä
of Canada   du Canada

MOSAIC PRESS
1252 Speers Road, Units 1 & 2
Oakville, Ontario L6L 5N9
phone: (905) 825-2130

info@mosaic-press.com

CONTENTS

A Girl and a Dove 11
All Good Things Thrown Away 33
Her Name is Egypt 49
First Crusade 67
Moses the Black 87
Breathe Life 107
A Face Like the Moon 143
Epilogue 155

For the 21.

"No tree, it is said, can grow to heaven unless it's roots reach down to hell."
- Carl Jung

A GIRL AND A DOVE

Nijma rode on her father's donkey, Shusho, in the dry heat of the early morning. Her father walked beside her holding a long stick he used to whip Shusho towards Mr. Shokry's farm.

Women in long cotton dresses and headscarves hung down to their waists balancing baskets of bread or produce on their heads and young light skinned and dark skinned girls holding on to their mother's thighs with small buckets in their hands, half full with fish or eggs or water, walked past Nijma and her father and his donkey to and from the old well up ahead. A young boy, maybe fifteen years old, drove a dirty white pickup full of watermelon and red and blue and green jerry cans with scratched silver patches down the dusty path. His mother sat in the passenger seat nursing a fat baby.

"Baba, how far is Mr. Shokry's farm?" Nijma asked. Today would be her first day at her new job.

"Another five minutes," her father said.

"Is Mr. Shokry a nice man?"

Her father licked his lips searching for an answer.

"He can be," he said and nodded, though he seemed unsteady. He'd been jittery all morning. "I think, maybe, I think you need to be honest with him. And he'll be honest with you."

Nijma didn't know what her father was talking about. She didn't ask if he was honest.

Nijma looked down at Shusho. He took his master's whips with a simple neigh and obeyed. She leaned down towards Shusho's fur and hugged his neck. The line of hair that ran from his head to his back brushed her cheeks.

A warm breeze kissed the back of her neck. She pushed herself up from Shusho. She wondered where the world ended and where the wind blew and if the wind itself knew. Wherever it went, she wished she could be. Anywhere but here.

She looked to the sky, blue and huge and everywhere in every corner of empty space. It was almost too big for her. But back down, just a few metres away on the crest of a pointed straw roof, a copper-winged dove sat and watched the streets move, cocking its head back and forth between the people and places below it. It pecked at its breast for a moment and chirped a quiet song. Only Nijma heard it. Perched above everyone, it stretched its wings to the clouds and flew off with the wind. Something in Nijma's soul melted. She smiled like she'd moved into a dream.

"I want a dove," she said.

Her father turned his head towards her and laughed.

"My simple little girl," he smiled and sighed and patted her back. "You don't know the world," he said.

A group of young boys kicked a rolled up ball of socks around a cluster of palm trees on the side of the road a few metres away. Nijma recognized the one with the big square head and glasses. He ran after the other boys like a drunk. The boy looked much older than the rest, twenty or so. The other boys were in their early teens. They yelled *keep away from the idiot* as they kicked to each other.

Nijma remembered the day her mother took her to the souq to buy fish, about a month earlier. She gave Nijma a few piasters and told her to buy a basket from the other side of the open air market while she haggled with the fish lady. "If she doesn't take what you give her, we don't need a new basket," her mother said.

Nijma nodded and walked away. It didn't take long before she realized she was lost. She could have turned around and told her mother she couldn't find anyone selling baskets, but Nijma needed to show her mother she could be trusted. She was almost seven.

She stood beside a papyrus plant at the edge of her village and examined the scattered tables. She saw merchants selling bundles of arugula, taro, herbs and spices, tomatoes and cabbage and lettuce and parsley, galabeyas and head scarves and bags made of straw and even underwear. But she couldn't find any baskets.

Nijma stepped away to keep searching but something dragged on her dress from the back and pulled her towards the papyrus, lifting her dress. Whatever had her let her go a second later. She heard something ruffle its feathers and squawk underneath her dress. The thing she didn't know flapped its wings against her legs and pecked at her ankle in frustration.

Nijma screamed and ran and tripped to the ground over her own feet. The thing formed a small tent under her dress and flapped its wings trying to find its way out from underneath, all the while shrieking and pecking at any skin that got in its way. Nijma pushed the creature out with her hands and cried. A small chicken popped its head from underneath her dress, squealed, raised its wings, and hopped away. From far, she looked like she gave birth to a chicken.

A boy with a big head and thick square glasses walked out from behind Nijma, laughing.

"You are, you are s-s-so retarded," he said, as he reached down for his hysterical chicken. "You are so, you are s-, retarded."

She wiped at her tears and reached for the end of her dress. A clump of crimson sand grew drop by drop beneath her bleeding ankle. She looked up at the old boy, his eyes narrow and slanted beneath his glasses. Skinny and short and dark with a neck almost as thick as his fat head.

"You are, I can't believe, you are so-"

A moustached man in a white skullcap slapped the boy down

with his open palm, forcing the chicken out of his hands. The boy's cheek turned red and his eyes misted. He held his red cheek with one hand and reached for the chicken with the other.

"You retard!" the man yelled. "You put a chicken under a five year old's dress you retard?"

The old boy stood up quickly.

"I-I'm not ree-, reet, she's retarded! She, she can't handle a chicken la-like a retard!"

The man shook his head and reached for Nijma's hand. She stuck it out reluctantly, though she hated that man for being the father of the idiot that attacked her. She wanted to hit him. She wanted to throw sand in his face, the stupid man and his stupid son, and spit on them. Instead, she gave him her hand.

"I'm sorry for my boy," the old man said as he pulled her up. "He's just retarded. He can't help it."

"I'm not retarded!" the boy cried. He dug his face into the feathers of his clucking chicken.

Nijma pushed the man off her and limped away as fast as she could. She had no basket, no chicken, and no piasters left in her palm. She must've dropped them during the chicken attack. What she did get that night was a beating by her father from the heel of his sandals. She deserved it for losing his money.

~~~

Nijma grew scared after seeing the big headed boy again.

"Go faster," she whispered into Shusho's ear.

A minute after they passed the well and walked out of the village, Nijma noticed a large mudbrick home two stories tall. Its walls were plastered and coloured blue, and a map of the Hajj, the owner's pilgrimage to Mecca, was drawn out on his door. A skinny man in a grey galabeya stood on a wooden burden behind two yoked water buffalo. He whipped them to work while he spoke on his cellphone.

"Is that Mr. Shokry's house?"

"Yes."

"Is that Mr. Shokry on that plough?"

"No. That's one of his workers. You'll meet Shokry eventually."

Nijma's father whipped Shusho to a small wooden stable. He carried his daughter off the donkey and walked out of the stable with her hand in his, and closed the wooden gate.

He led her through a wide grass field cut through by lines of mud and dust towards two mudbrick houses a few kilometres away. Both were similar in size and shape. Their doors were made of long planks of scratched, worn wood. Each had a small rectangular window eight feet above their door, though one was covered in tinted glass and the other had no glass. They stood a few metres apart.

As they approached, a skinny man in jeans and a pompadour walked out of the house with the glass window and towards the other house. He looked well rested, relaxed, and his Western clothes and greased hair made him look rich to Nijma.

"Is that Mr. Shokry?" she asked.

"No," he said. "Shokry is in the other home. The one the man's walking towards."

"What did that guy do in there?"

Her father kept quiet for a moment. He released her hand and raised his own above her head and patted her. She looked up at him. His dark eyes completely lifeless, tired, as if he'd worn out his answer to that question so many times before. Whatever was in that house, he couldn't justify.

"Doctor, but a special kind of doctor," he said. "Only for men. Not little girls."

"What kind of doctor is that?"

"A man's doctor. Girls go to girl's doctors, boys go to boy's doctors."

They arrived at the home with the open window and knocked

on the door. Nijma heard a man stagger and thump towards her. He swung the door open. Nijma looked up. Six feet from the floor, the man was the tallest Egyptian she'd ever seen. And fat, his stomach poking through his galabeya like a pregnant woman, with bright brown eyes and a moustache that stretched from one cheek to the other, curled at its ends.

"Oh sweet sweet day," the fat man roared with a smile. "We have an angel at the door."

The little girl smiled a shy smile and moved her eyes between his face and the doorpost, she was so shy.

"Hi," she said rubbing her arm. "It's nice to meet you."

"It's my pleasure," he said and extended his arm inside the little home.

"Leave the money on the table and get out," he hollered at the man with the pompadour staring at a papyrus print of Isis. The man cursed under his breath and threw his money on an orange table and marched out. He stared at the little girl as if surprised. Nijma stepped to the side as he left, then walked into the fat man's house.

"Remember," her father whispered to the fat man, "she cleans, she polishes, she scrubs, she wipes, she picks corn and cotton. She can make simple food. That's it."

The fat man shook his head and smiled. "I remember."

"No visits to the doctor," he said motioning his head towards the other house. "You promised me she wouldn't become a doctor herself." Nijma watched her father's eyes open wide as he spoke. She knew he was scared. She was scared too. This job was important to her, her father and mother. They needed the money.

"Doctors, is that what you call them?" the fat man laughed. "A promise is a promise sir." He shook his head and smiled. He looked honest.

Her father nodded, patted his chest, and walked away to the fat man's field where he worked.

The fat man slammed the door shut and walked towards the

girl.

"Don't worry," he winked, "you can be whatever you want someday. Even a doctor."

She examined his little house. Pages and pages of papers were scattered on a small desk at the far corner of the room.

A large wooden hutch stood across from it filled with bowls and sifters, cups, grinders, bags of flour and wheat and knives. The orange table in the middle of the room carried the pompadour man's money, a nail clipper, a cabbage and a raw slab of beef beside a mallet. A gas oven faced the table.

"I was gonna ask you to bake me some bread, but I already started on the meat. You ever make meat before?"

Nijma shook her head. She'd rarely seen meat at her own home, except for the occasional engagement or wedding.

"I just need you to bang that hammer looking thing on the piece of meat as hard as you can until it becomes nice and soft. Then I'll do the rest and you can make the bread. I'd do it myself but I have some work to do."

"What are you gonna do?"

"I'll show you after," he said, and walked to his desk. Nijma walked over to the little table, it only stood a foot and a half from the ground. She sat on the floor in front of it, picked up the mallet with both hands, and beat the piece of meat with all the little strength she could muster. She grew tired within a few minutes.

Nijma picked up the piece of meat and waved it in her hand. It seemed pretty soft, but she didn't know if it was actually ready or not. She had no memory of making meat she could compare it to.

"Mr. Shokry," she said, "I think it's done."

"Good," he said, keeping his eyes on the paper in front of him. "See that brown tray on the stove?"

"Yes."

"Put the meat in the tray and put the tray in the oven. It's already hot. Then come here. I wanna show you some of my work."

She did what the man asked her. She squirmed from the heat

as she placed the tray in the oven. Nijma walked over to his desk. He looked back at her and smiled. From close, he smelled like sweat and grass.

He put down the pencil and organized the papers in his hand, making sure they were in order, then placed them back on the desk. He reached for the little girl and pulled her up to his lap. She'd never sat on the lap of a man she wasn't related to before. She felt something dirty grow in her stomach. Her shoulders rolled into her body and her muscles tensed. She tried to wriggle off his lap, quietly.

"Whoa!" he smiled and gently pulled her stomach towards him.

"I'm your uncle," he said. "You don't love your own uncle?"

"No your-"

"Sure I am! Your baba didn't tell you?"

"No." She stared at him wide-eyed.

"Oh. Maybe he doesn't know then. But I know. And now you know." He smirked and squeezed her cheeks.

"Don't tell him though. It'll be our little secret," he winked. She realized no matter how much she squirmed, he wouldn't let her go. So she sat.

His lap was hot. Nijma felt him all around her, but she wouldn't look at him. She slowed her breathing — she didn't want to take in his stench all at once. And she needed to talk to him. She needed him to know that she liked him, even though she didn't. It could be the only way she could get off his lap.

Mr. Shokry turned towards his desk. He pointed to a sketch of a faceless girl in front of him. She wore a short sleeve t-shirt and pants.

How odd. Maybe it wasn't a girl, though the curves on the drawing suggested it was. It could've been a big breasted man.

"Is that a man or a woman?" Nijma asked.

"A woman. In America, the women wear pants, like men. But you can tell them apart by their body and their hair. And also the way they smell. They spend a lot of money to smell different."

"What is this on her t-shirt?"

"It says *Fashion*."

"*Fah-shun*?"

"It means something nice like a rose or watermelon. Something nice. What do you think? I think you like the drawing, don't you?"

"It's nice," she said. "But this *fashu* woman is confused. She feels like a man, with her pants."

Mr. Shokry pushed the girl off his lap. She landed on her feet and fell to the ground. She felt the tears well in her eyes, but she held her voice.

"You don't understand the future," he yelled. "It's coming and it'll pass you by, the way you think."

She wanted to walk away, but she was scared. So she rolled off her knees and onto her bottom. He sat in front of her. She looked at him for a moment. He sat facing his work. She turned her head to the ground and breathed. She wiped the tears from her eyes and sniffed. She hoped he didn't hear. But she heard him turn his chair. She saw him uncross his legs and lean forward. She felt him stare. He was hungry for something.

"I'm sorry," he said calmly. "I get angry sometimes."

Nijma nodded. He turned away towards his work. He picked up the picture of the woman in pants to the light and smiled.

"I'm thinking of one day sending this out to an American."

He turned towards Nijma.

"Yeah, maybe I'll try," he said flipping through his pages. He turned to her. "You have any dreams?"

She nodded.

"Well," he said. "What are they?"

She sighed. She knew she had to answer. She didn't want him to push her to the ground again. She knew she had to tell the truth. The fat man looked like he knew a lie too well.

"I wanna meet a nice dove," she said staring out the window.

"A dove?"

"Yes."

"Why a dove?"

"They know where the wind goes. They fly where the wind flies."

Shokry laughed a heavy laugh. She knew he would, just like her father did. He patted the girl on her head.

"Oh the dreams of a princess," he bellowed with a smile. "I think they have their own village somewhere close to the Sinai. Maybe they need to get back to their families. Doves have families too you know?"

Nijma sighed and nodded her head. She heard a few footsteps approach from outside and turned around. The door swung open and an older boy with a patchy beard walked in with a chubby woman. She was dressed in an all black, except for her orange headscarf that only covered the back half of her head, her dark thick hair streaked with lines of copper. Her cheeks were so fat, so round, like a child, and she was short.

The man was paying for his treatment, so this woman must've been the doctor. Nijma was stunned. She'd never seen a female doctor in her village before. Mr. Shokry wasn't lying. Maybe she would be a doctor someday, just like the lady in the orange headscarf. But she wouldn't work for Mr. Shokry, even if he was her uncle.

"How much do I owe you?" he asked before he spotted Mr. Shokry.

"Fifty on the table."

The young man spotted Nijma on his way to the table. He cocked his head back as he reached under his galabeya for his wallet.

"They just keep getting younger and younger don't they?" he said.

"She's not ready yet you animal," Shokry said. "Put your money on the table and get out."

"This is the girl?" the doctor yelled. Her accent wasn't from around here. She smiled and walked towards her. "She looks like old pictures of me when I was young."

"Really?" Shokry said as the boy was leaving. "Maybe I should give her back to her baba before she turns into you." He laughed. "And why didn't you come out with that dog with the pompadour? He could have left without giving me my money."

"He smelled like garbage. I couldn't stand another minute with him. I'm not gonna let him in next time."

"Money is money," Shokry said.

The doctor pulled the little girl towards the oven and sat on the floor beside her. "Stick out your palms," she said.

Nijma shook her head but the doctor forced her palm out from underneath her. "Look at that," she said running her finger down Nijma's lifeline. You've got a long long life ahead of you." Nijma didn't understand what was happening. But at least the doctor's words were good.

She stopped at an intersecting crease in her lifeline.

"There we go, there's the disaster," she said. "You live and you die at seventeen."

Nijma looked up at the doctor's eyes, confused, and tried to pull her hand away. The doctor wouldn't let go.

"Married at seventeen," she said. "Then another sixty years of slavery."

The doctor let Nijma's palm go.

"Nope. That's not the life for me," she said. "I was born alone and I'll die alone."

The doctor looked like she was approaching her thirties. Nijma had never seen or even heard of a woman that old still unmarried.

"You don't want a husband?" Nijma asked.

"Ha!" the doctor yelled. "So I can get on my knees every day and clean the crud off the floor? And carry tiny monsters in my stomach for a year and bear them for the rest of my life? Yeah you're right. I guess I'll just sell my soul to a garbage man and birth his garbage children."

"Don't be so indignant to the little girl you pig," Shokry hollered. "You've already sold your soul to me."

He stood up and pulled Nijma away from the doctor. "Sorry about Aisha. All those years in med school turned her a little crazy." He turned and winked at Aisha.

Aisha laughed. "Man after man after man. I don't know how many prescriptions I have left in me." She rolled up one of her sleeves and smoothed the hairs on her arm to one side. "It's a busy life," she hushed to herself.

Nijma heard someone knocking at the door. Shokry told her to go stand by the table and look as if she's cooking bread. He called for the people at the door to come in. Nijma heard the door crack open as she approached the hutch to fetch the flour. A man in a skullcap and moustache walked in with his big headed son. Nijma panicked and tried to hide herself behind the hutch, but she knew both had seen her already.

"Why's there a little girl here?" the man with the skullcap asked Shokry.

"In training," Shokry said. "Who's this?"

"My son."

"Why would you bring your son to a place like this?"

"I can't get him married," the man in the skullcap said. "This is the only way it'll happen."

"I d-, I don't w-wanna do this," the boy with the big head cried.

His father slapped him on the back of his neck and pointed his finger to the boy's face. "You may be retarded," the man whispered with such hostility, "But you're my son. My blood. You're a man. Do what men do."

The boy dropped to the floor and held his hands to his face and cried. His father shook his head, disgusted, and yelled at him to get up.

"Get the girl so we can finish this," he said to Shokry. Shokry waved his hands at Aisha, but she squinted her eyes and shook her head. She looked disgusted.

"Let's go," Shokry said. She shook her head again and looked away. Nijma wondered why she wouldn't treat the boy. He was obviously sick. She wondered why the boy didn't want to get better.

Shokry breathed a heavy breath and marched up to Aisha. She threw her arms over her face and tried to duck behind the table. With a slight smirk and a raised brow, he slapped her with a swift hand, the rage of the devil in his eyes. She fell on the dirty floor and laid there, her legs curled to her stomach. She grasped her cheek. Her whimper muffled by the stupid cry of the fat headed boy.

"What, you're disgusted by him because he's retarded?" the boy's father yelled. "You're a whore!"

Aisha crawled away from Shokry's feet and stood up. She ran out of the house cursing under her breath. The man in the skullcap picked his son up off the floor, pushed him out the door and followed her.

"Suh-s-save me chicken girl!" the boy cried, reaching one hand out to Nijma. His eyes were wide like the sun and the darkest black. She saw his tears and she remembered her own. She saw him struggle as his father heaved him out of the home and followed Aisha, slamming the door closed behind him. He writhed like she did when she tried to squirm off the fat man's lap. She wondered if she was retarded.

Nijma held the bag of flour between her arms in a corner of the room. She held it close and clenched at its fabric, eyes and lips open.

"What's a whore?" she asked Mr. Shokry.

Shokry turned to face the young girl. "She's a doctor, I told you. She helps men feel better."

He turned back around and walked to his desk and sat.

"You hit her," she said, not surprised, but very scared. The man moved between rage and peace by the grace of his open palm.

"Money is money," he shrugged.

Nijma sat quietly and stared at the man. He was sketching again. He smirked. He almost always smirked. Even as he hit Aisha, he smirked, though his eyes looked different at the time. Now he looked calm. All that he cared for at that moment was the piece of paper that lay in front of him.

She stood up and dragged the flour bag to the small table. She got a few extra ingredients from the hutch and began making sun bread. The two hardly spoke a word between each other for the rest of the day. He took the meat out of the oven himself and told her he'd eat it with his wife in his blue home where he'd spend the rest of the day. He needed her to tell Aisha to take the names of her patients as they left, just in case they didn't pay. Nijma told her when she came back. He also needed to redirect the patients to the blue house to see him before they saw Aisha.

Nijma made the dough, kneaded it, and set it out in the sun to rise. She didn't make many loaves. Maybe ten in all. Her hands were too small to be productive. She spent most of the time sitting outside, waiting for men to pass through. She told them to report to the blue house first and watched the bread rise. She also watched the birds fly above her, land, and peck around the grass and dirt floor for food. Most of them were pigeons. She didn't care much for pigeons. She even ate them. Pigeon meat was expensive, but not like meat.

But every once in a while, she'd spot a dove. Beige underbelly, copper wings that faded to a light blue at their tips. They were beautiful. They flew with a grace pigeons lacked, as if they didn't fly at all, but glided.

She tried that afternoon to sneak up behind one. It spotted her, waddled away stretching its wings, and flew off into the sky. At least she figured out where they went that day. To a far off village in the Sinai to be with their families.

By the time the bread rose, Nijma realized her day had almost passed. She gathered the risen pieces of dough on a large tray and moved them inside. She decided not to put them in the oven since she didn't know how to turn it on. A few minutes later, she heard someone open the door.

Mr. Shokry walked in. And scurrying behind him, a bird. Its copper wings faded to blue at its ends.

A dove! Nijma thought when she saw it, though she didn't say it out loud. Nijma noticed the big smile on Mr. Shokry's face. Maybe hers was infectious.

The bird raised its wings and tried to fly away but couldn't. One of its legs was tied to a short string that Shokry held in his hand by the opposite end.

"Where did you get that?" she beamed.

"I have a pigeon coop on the farm. Sometimes I find doves. You like it?"

"Yes!"

"You want it?"

Nijma looked up at the man, smirking as always, then back down at the dove, which tried and tried but couldn't fly away. It stood at his legs, shifting its head from one side to the other. She walked towards Shokry and reached and grabbed the string out of his hand.

"Thank you," she said.

"See you tomorrow?"

"Yes."

She walked out of the house and towards the stable where Shusho stood.

"I need to name you," she said. She spotted her father under the stable. He waved her down.

"Look what I have," she smiled.

"How'd you get that?" her father asked.

Nijma explained to him that she didn't catch it. Mr. Shokry gave it to her and she wanted to name it. Nijma picked the dove up into her arms and her father threw her onto Shusho. She petted him from the top of its head down to his back, but she could feel him try to stretch his wings and fly away. She wondered why he wanted to leave her. She loved the dove, her only dove. She might never have another in her arms again. She named him Mahboub, or Beloved, and promised she'd feed him and play with him and do whatever she needed to do to keep him happy.

Mahboub and Nijma rode home on Shusho that night. Nijma's father walked beside them, whipping Shusho along. At half past six, the sun ducked its top beneath the approaching horizon. The day's light faded to a dim orange that reminded Nijma of Aisha's headscarf.

In her mind, she hadn't decided whether she thought Aisha was beautiful or not. She was so portly and small, like a fat child. Her hair grew down to her chest, long and wavy, just like Nijma's. And her dark brown eyes, even when she smiled, she didn't look happy. Like Nijma, she was born alone. But unlike Nijma, Aisha would die alone. At least according to Aisha's prophecy.

Mahboub tried to fly away. Even though Nijma held his string, he tried and tried again.

When they got home, Nijma took a few pieces of bread she'd stuffed in her head scarf and tried to feed them to him. He pecked at the bread on the floor, turned around, flapped his wings and tried to scratch the string off one of his legs with the other. Nijma sang Little Duckie Nunu with Mahboub, but he wouldn't whistle back.

She tied him to a post at a far corner in her house and petted him.

"Did baba get that for you?" her mother asked her.

"No mama," Nijma said. "Mr. Shokry gave it to me."

Her mother's lips cringed at the sound of the fat man's name. She shook her head and walked to the stove. She poured some molokhiya into a bowl, the soup spilled like green mucous, placed it on a tray with some sun bread, and brought it to her husband who sat on the floor. She laid it in front of him and stood in front of him watching him eat. Nijma stood beside her.

"Sit," he said not looking up at them.

They sat and broke off a piece of sun bread and dipped it in the soup.

"When do you want me to make that dove?" her mother asked.

"No mama!" Nijma cried. "It's not for-"

"Nijma!" her dad yelled punching the ground. "Don't ever yell at your mother!"

Nijma ducked her head to the food and broke off another piece of bread.

"It's Nijma's bird," her father said. "She can do what she wants with it."

Her mother nodded. Nijma ate fast and she finished within a few minutes. Her parents were not yet done. She asked if she could go outside with Mahboub for a while. Her father let her go. She untied the bird and walked out. She stood in front of her home below a window. She could hear her parents talking inside while she watched Mahboub.

"We can't keep her with that man," her mother said.

"She's only helping him around the house. He promised me."

"How can you trust a man like that," her voice raised, cautiously. Nijma wondered what she was talking about.

"He's not a liar."

Nobody spoke for a while. Nijma tried to feed Mahboub some pebbles to weigh him down so he wouldn't fly away. He wouldn't have it. She massaged his little head. He shook her off and flapped his wings.

"Do you not have any shame?" she heard her mother say. "Where is your honour?" Nijma heard the slap. It wasn't particularly loud. She shuffled away as fast as she could so her dove wouldn't hear. She and Mahboub were going for a short walk.

So many people around the village told her how beautiful her bird was. Many asked when she'd eat it. To that, she blew them raspberries, picked up her bird and covered his ears, and walked away. Some didn't mind, others cursed at her, but she didn't care. She was bold for his sake. But still, Mahboub tried to fly.

At night, after her mother told her to get to sleep, she climbed a ladder to her roof with a small hand towel covering Mahboub in her left hand. She placed the string that held his leg under a brick she found on her roof. From far, she could see the lights from passing ships slowly guide her eyes down the Nile. She usually slept within minutes of the first owl's hoot. It had already been a half hour and she couldn't fall asleep.

"Why do you want to leave me?" she said, adjusting the hand towel around Mahboub's back.

You think I do but I don't he said. *We're friends. I'm happy I met you.*

"Then why didn't you eat the bread and the pebbles I gave you? I put them right there in front of you."

I wasn't hungry Nijma. I ate enough grass in the day.

"Well why didn't you whistle with me when I sang to you? You didn't like the song?"

I love that song. Little duckie Nunu, You lost your little shoe shoe, When you walked around you stepped on some doodoo. Nijma sang the song along with Mahboub.

"Why didn't you whistle then?"

My mouth was tired. I've been whistling all day.

"So you don't want to leave me? You've been trying to fly away since I met you."

I have a family Nijma. I have a wife and a hundred children and all my friends are in the Sinai. They miss me. They don't even know where I am now.

"So, you want to leave me. For your family?"

I'll never leave you he said. *You'll see me and I'll see you. And when you don't see me I'll see you and I'll be there.*

With that, Mahboub fluffed his feathers, turned his head and buried his beak in the down on his back, knocking the hand towel off of him. He shut his little eyes and slept standing on the brick that weighed him to her roof.

"If in the morning, you want to leave," Nijma said pulling the string from underneath the brick, "I'll understand."

She crawled a few steps over to the blanket she slept under every night, pulled it over her, and turned to Mahboub. "Goodnight," she said, and closed her eyes.

The weight of the sun's light beat on her olive eyelids the next morning. She opened her eyes and yawned and stretched her arms out to the light. She sat up and turned towards where Mahboub had slept the night before. There, in front of her, sat a brick. No string. No dove. A brick.

Nijma felt the dull impact of the sun move down from her head to her chest to the core of her stomach. That moment, she knew Aisha's prophecy was wrong. At the birth of a new day, she'd lost her love to the Sinai. She never would have lost him if she hadn't given him his freedom. She was stupid to think he would have stayed. She put her hands to her face and whimpered. No one heard.

Aisha would understand. She probably cried on the floor all the time.

Nijma heard her dad call her from the ground. She breathed, wiped her eyes with her sleeves, and climbed down the ladder. She washed her face in a bowl of water and brushed her teeth with an old brush she'd gotten as charity. She changed her galabeya from the night before, she'd already worn it for a few days, and walked out to her father standing beside Shusho. He said good morning and she said good morning and he threw her on top of Shusho. He whipped Shusho's backside and they made their way through the village.

"Where's your little bird friend?"

"With his family," she muttered.

"He escaped?"

"I think so."

Not a word was spoken for the rest of the trip.

Her father dropped her off at the mudbrick house with no glass. Shokry smiled and let her in.

"I have something to show you," he said, tugging her little hand to one end of the room, his other hand holding the mallet Nijma had used to tenderize his meat the day before. She knew she'd have to cook again.

Aisha sat on the floor smoking a cigarette, this time in a bright blue galabeya. A long multicoloured galabeya hung from a small coat-rack in the corner of the room. The end of the galabeya was cut down the middle and sewn into two parts, turning it into pants. The sewing was shoddy, but strong enough to hold. Long green stripes ran down the length of each sleeve and pant leg. "My creation," he called it.

"I made it with a few of my wife's old dresses. What do you think?"

She examined it up and down, held it in her hands, touched its seams. She wondered, if she still had Mahboub, and the galabeya was much smaller, would he wear it? He'd be the only one among his friends and family with a galabeya. He'd look so good.

"I like it," she said. "It's beautiful."

He turned to his creation and smiled.

"It is," he said. "It is beautiful. I made a beautiful thing."

Nijma heard someone open the door. She turned, and saw the man with the pompadour walk in. He wore jeans and a t-shirt.

"Tariq!" Mr. Shokry said. "Come look at this."

Tariq walked to where the girl stood, looked down at her confused, and up at the altered galabeya.

"What is this?" he asked. "Where'd you get this? The circus?" Tariq laughed and brushed his hand through his pompadour. Shokry turned to him, amazed. Nijma heard Aisha giggle in the corner, although she tried not to.

"Did your buffalo make this?" He looked down again at Nijma. He patted her head and slid her scarf partially off. He ran his hands through her hair. She tried to push his hands off, but he persisted and grinned. He looked up at Shokry.

"How much for the little girl?"

"I'm not a doctor," she said. He laughed and stared at Shokry. "Doctor?"

Before Nijma could see him wind up, she saw his mallet hit Tariq's face. Tariq fell to the ground, eyes open, bleeding from his nose and his mouth, a slight dent on his bloodied skull. He didn't move. A small yelp squeaked out of Aisha's mouth.

Nijma breathed heavily but tried to stay quiet. She felt her feet plant to the floor by the fear that if she moved, she'd lie next to Tariq. Shokry turned to Nijma. He stepped towards Aisha, who sat on the floor licking her lips and looking at the wall. He sat on a seat that hovered above her and stared at Nijma.

"Cigarette," he said. Nijma assumed he was talking to Aisha, but he was looking at Nijma. Aisha kept her sight to the wall as she reached for one from her pack, lit it, and passed it to him. His hand trembled as he reached for the cigarette. He stared at the little girl and blew smoke from his nostrils.

"You liked it?" he said, calmly. He wasn't smiling.

"Yes!" she yelled in an honest panic. "It's really pretty! I love it!"

He nodded and ran a hand through his moustache. The fat man crossed his legs and looked at Aisha, crouched against the wall. She looked like a wave in her blue dress. He turned back to Nijma.

"This," he said pointing to Aisha with his cigarette. "This is a doctor. She's old. She's not afraid to risk her life. She's smart. She's given her life to her work. Not to any one man. Not to any bird."

Nijma lowered her head to the ground when he brought up Mahboub.

"Mahboub is gone," she said. "I loved him and he left me."

The fat man laughed.

"You lost my bird?" he asked. "I gave you one bird, and you lost it?"

She didn't answer. It was never his bird. He never loved Mahboub like she loved him. The fat man didn't even know his name.

"You think you're smart?" he asked.

She shook her head no.

"Of course you're not. You're a peasant girl. You're the daughter of a farmer, a *Nazarene*, with no land. What money can I make off you?" he said with sharp eyes.

He leaned forward and looked her in her eyes.

"You will never be a doctor," he hushed, a forced calm in his stare. "You will never work for me. I never want to see you in this house again. I never want to see you close to Aisha again. You will never end up like her. Understand?"

She nodded her head, her heart pulsing against her flesh.

"Leave. And tell your father he's gone too."

Nijma ran out of the house as fast as she could towards the field her father worked. She found him feeding Shokry's water buffalo in the stable next to Shusho. She told him the bad news in tears. She watched his face turn red and his eyes swell with rage. He stood for a few seconds staring at his daughter. Just as quickly as it had come, his face turned its normal colour. He leaned on the gate and breathed. He laughed.

"Everything'll be alright," he said. He ran a hand through his hair and picked up his daughter. She cried on his shoulder. He patted her back. A new feeling began to grow in her. Something like happiness. Maybe not happiness. Maybe comfort. Like how she felt when she was with Mahboub. She sniffed and wondered how he was doing. How his family and friends were. She wondered if he thought about her. He said he'd be with her always. He was watching. She could feel him with her. He built a little nest in her heart.

ALL GOOD THINGS THROWN AWAY

I laid my hands above the cold sink that early morning. My head hovered above the drain. I raised it slowly but I was tired. I looked at myself in the mirror that rested against the grey wall in front of me and stared for a moment trying to wake, my face cut through the middle by a crack that ran through the glass. Concrete walls stood above and all around me. *All that's missing is bars* I thought. My eyes were barely open and still red in the dim light. My hair stuck out on one side. I combed it down with my hands.

And there I was. Still fat. A hippo in a shallow lake of garbage.

I showered under a garden hose and brushed my teeth and dressed in a pair of plain grey track pants I brought from Canada and a green Abibas sweater giddu gave me as a welcome gift. *Nothing here is legitimate* I thought when he stretched it out in front of me, smiling like it was the real thing. I doubt he was able to read English anyway. That was his excuse. Mine? A shirt was a shirt.

I walked out of the bathroom and heard the cock crow. The same cock that woke me twenty minutes earlier. It might've been just after two in the morning now.

I dragged myself towards the door and accidentally kicked something furry and small on my way out. I curled my toes against the cold cracked tiles and looked down. I screamed like a girl when I saw that it was a mouse, but it was dead. All I could see of it in the little light in the room was that it was dark grey and hunched towards its legs. It laid still on its side with its mouth open like it had something to say before it died.

This was Moqattam, Egypt's Garbage City. It smelled a lot worse last night when I'd arrived. Like meat left out in the sun for too long. It was hard to breathe for the first hour and the garbage was everywhere. On the streets and on the roofs and in the shops and at the city gates. None of it seemed real. Walking around this city, I felt like I was floating. Like everything I saw and smelled and touched was another boy's senses.

I wished I was back home in Canada in my single garage house with AC. But if not that, I wished I could've at least stayed with my parents in New Cairo and attended the wedding with them. But my mom told me giddu missed me. He hadn't seen me since I was three years old. That was almost twelve years ago.

I toed around a pile of Pert Plus bottles in the middle of giddu's living room and made my way out of his apartment.

He sat on a dirty wooden chair to the side of his redbrick home inhaling smoke from a shisha and blowing billows out his nose.

"Give me a second," he said between breaths and put his mouth back to the pipe.

He looked a lot like mom. Big square head. Dark brown skin. But unlike my mom, he had sharp narrow eyes and a moustache that cut off on each side of his upper lip. He still had most of his hair, except for a little bird's nest at the back of his head. And he always wore one of his several grey galabeyas.

I walked across from where he sat to his white Chevy pickup, probably early nineties, possibly the only clean thing in Moqattam. It gleamed in the moonlight. I leaned against its door.

"Whoa!" giddu bellowed throwing down the mouth end of the shisha's hose and brushing his hand in the air as if to say get off. I walked away from his truck wondering what I'd done wrong.

"Everything but the truck," he said as he got up and walked towards me. He had a spry step too agile for a man well into his sixties. "You don't lean on a Chevy my friend," he said. "It's American, like you."

"I'm from Canada."

"What's the difference? America is America," he said and took out a cloth from a pocket stitched into the front of his galabeya. He wiped down the place I'd leaned on.

"I just washed her last night and you stick your butt on her like you're George Bush?"

"I'm not American."

"Semina doesn't need that from you Mr. Bush. I'm her president. She takes me where I need to go."

Semina, his car, or Fat Girl in English.

"Now get in," he said, unlocking the passenger door and walking towards his shisha to put it out.

Giddu stepped in himself a moment later. He pulled out a small, square piece of paper from the glove compartment in front of me, rolled it up into a thin cone and put it to his mouth. He pretended to smoke it even though it wasn't lit and put the car in first gear and drove off.

He'd been smoking his paper since the moment he'd seen me just yesterday. His eyes wide as he walked towards me and hugged me, but he didn't take the paper out until he kissed me, and it went back in as he hovered over me afterwards.

"*Me no smoke*," he said in his best English. I assumed he meant he didn't smoke cigarettes. He just puffed on a piece of unlit paper.

My mother told him I could speak Arabic. He laughed and hugged and kissed his youngest daughter, my mother, and greeted me in Arabic.

Back in his Chevy, we passed row after row of short brown and redbrick buildings. Piles of unsorted bottles and newspapers and banana peels and melon rinds and other garbage were scattered on the ground from days before. The world in front of me was mortar and ash and uneven stonework under a still, concrete skyline.

Two boys in a buggy pulled by a pair of mules rode behind us. A large empty bin covered by a tarp rested at the back of their buggy. I looked back at giddu beside me, still smoking his paper.

"Why do you do that?" I asked.

"Do what?" he spoke through his teeth, not letting the paper fall from his lips.

"Smoke that paper. You don't even light it. Why don't you just buy some cigarettes?"

"I used to smoke two packs a day my friend. Two packs. Until a doctor I met at church told me I'd go impotent. You know what that is? Impotence?"

"No."

"How old are you now?"

"Fourteen."

"You're not that young. You should know what it means. It means you can't have kids." He took the paper from out his mouth and breathed out. "I said 'what? Can't have kids? Who will take care of my business when I'm gone?' So I decided I was gonna quit."

"So you just quit?"

"I must've failed a million times. I kept buying packs and smoking them. I didn't think it would be that hard. Remember, this was thirty years ago. What was it like a few pennies for a pack? So one day after I bought another pack, I said to myself, 'you bought it, you eat it.' And I ate my cigarette."

"What?" I said hitting my head against the back of my seat.

"Lord knows," he shook his head. "I chewed it right up and swallowed. It was like eating fire. I didn't crave another cigarette for another hour. And I ate the next one too. And the one after that. Every time I wanted a cigarette, I sat down and ate one. I felt like an ashtray. You know how long I did that for? A good month. God knows it was the best thing for me. Look how many kids I had after that. Samir," he said sticking out his thumb, starting the count.

"Saif, Souheir, Marwan, Sausan." At five, he moved onto his other hand.

"Salim, Shakira, Sahra, George, your mother Salima, Philo, how much is that now?"

"Eleven," I said, half-amazed, still tired.

"Eleven," he smirked and sat back in his seat. "I did it."

"You smoke shisha though."

"The doctor said cigarettes. Not shisha."

"Oh. You still didn't tell me why you pretend to smoke paper."

"I need something in my mouth at all times," he said taking a puff. "I feel naked without it."

I shrugged my shoulders and watched as we passed the makeshift gates made of garbage at the border of Moqattam. This was my first garbage run with my grandpa. I was not excited.

I sat there listening to giddu tell me stories of past garbage runs where he ran into an old village friend or found a gold ring among the waste or the time he scavenged the street he'd been working for thirty years in just under forty-five minutes, his all time record. I shook my head and tried to care.

We got to Cairo after the longest twenty minute drive I could remember. We stopped in front of a grey building a few stories high. I rolled down the window. It was cold out, lit only by a dim light from a lamp at the end of the short street.

"I used to do half this street," Giddu said as he climbed out. "But as the boys grew, I got more and more workers in my workforce. And now I own this whole street!"

"Nobody's here but us," I said.

"Saif and Marwan will be here in another hour."

"How much do you do by yourself?" I asked.

"Just this building," he winked. "See what happens when you stop smoking?"

I nodded and followed him to the back of his pickup. He took an extra wheelbarrow for me that day, a small black one. Smaller than his at least, which was almost the size of my bathtub back home. I followed him into the building. We took the elevator up to the top floor. There were five floors, five apartments per floor. Not all of them had garbage in front of their doors, though most did.

Giddu threw the bags into his barrow like a man who'd never seen a loss. He sometimes stopped to look inside the bag before he threw it in the barrow. The first time he did it, he shook his head as if amazed.

"All good things thrown away," he said running his hands through the garbage. I cringed, although the bag wasn't filled with much more than plastics and paper. He tied the bag back up and threw it on the pile and he marched on. I lugged my barrow behind him and waited for him to throw bags in it.

We finished pretty quickly, giddu said because he had me as a helper, and made our way out of the building. Giddu walked with a slight bounce and a tired smile. Giddu opened the back gate of his pickup and pulled out a wide wooden plank. He rested one side of the plank on the edge of the pickup's gate and the other down to the asphalt. He rolled his barrow up the plank first and let it fall on its side once it was up there, letting the garbage spill. He did the same with my barrow and told me to get back in the truck.

"So are you getting married soon or what?" Giddu asked on our way back to Moqattam.

"I told you, I'm fourteen."

"So?"

"So, I'm too young."

"Are you joking or what? You're joking right? I married your tayta when she was fifteen. She bore me eleven kids, and I was poor as dirt. But you," he said turning to me and nodding, his eyes smiling. "A boy as fat as you can get any woman he wants."

He turned his head back to the road. I felt my face flush and clenched my fist. I looked over at giddu, a new rolled paper in his mouth, narrowed eyes staring at the road. He almost looked like he meant it. I breathed out and relaxed my palm and placed it on my lap.

"She was fifteen," he said, "I was nineteen. If you start early, you could beat me. You could beat eleven."

"I don't want to beat eleven. And I don't want to get married anytime soon."

"Yes you do."

"No I don't."

"You're telling me there's not one girl back home you're interested in?"

"No."

I lied. But the girl I liked didn't share my giddu's opinions on fatness.

Cindy Thomas.

Little Miss skinny Cindy and her wide blue eyes. She brought in her tiara one time after she'd won her first pageant. All the girls were jealous and a few of the boys started teasing her to get her attention. She shrugged them off like flies. A fly could never touch her perfect skin.

"What'd you do to win that?" I asked her the day she walked into school with the tiara on her head.

"I tried not to spend the few dollars I had on Big Macs everyday like you fatty," she smirked. A few of her friends broke out in laughter along with her on cue. I always wondered why they hated her behind her back and sucked up to her in her face.

"Go back to the ghetto," she chirped and turned around to talk to the girls she owned. They stopped noticing me, and I stopped existing.

I forgot everything in that moment and wished I could destroy her. I reached for my left shoe, nobody paid me any attention. I took it off after a short struggle with my laces and whipped it at her face, hit her in the nose with my tattered Reebok. She fell to the ground holding her nose, her tiara lying on the asphalt by her side on the school courtyard, and cried.

A few minutes later, I sat in the principal's office waiting for my mother to come pick me up on the first day of my suspension. I remembered how the shoe hit her face and how she fell and I hated her and her tiara and wished I could say sorry in a place we were all alone and she'd accept and reach for my hand.

"No girl yet," I told giddu.

"Don't worry," he said. "She'll come soon, God willing."

We pulled in through the gates of Moqattam after about twenty minutes. The sun, now awake, peeked its head above the horizon. Several pickups and buggies with garbage pyramids on their backs made their way through the narrow village lanes. Just barely five in the morning, a short round man with a thick curled moustache that could've reached his eyes if he stretched it opened up the doors to his coffee shop.

A crude painting on the side of the man's door of the Virgin in a blue cloak carrying baby Jesus caught me. She stared at the village streets and the passing crowds, smiling. But she didn't look happy. Just content. The streets were full and everyone was too busy living to care that they lived in garbage. She held her baby and watched everything move like a well-oiled machine.

I thanked God my mother managed to get out when she could. When she was twelve, she moved in with her eldest brother who owned a small pawn shop on the outskirts of downtown Cairo where he slept. My mother told me giddu let her leave so she could get an education – he had enough daughters to sort his garbage. One less mouth to feed for giddu. He put that responsibility on his son who made more than enough money for the both of them.

Giddu rolled on down the dirt road and we passed the short round man and his coffee shop. We stopped in front of giddu's building, his shisha still standing where he left it, and walked out of the car. I followed giddu to the back of his truck. He climbed up the tailgate, rolled the barrows down the plank, and told me to stay beside them. He tossed the bags of garbage at me. I dodged the first one. I could smell it coming.

"What are you doing?" giddu roared with a half smile like he was half joking. "Pick it up and throw it in the barrow."

I did what he said and I didn't let any of the other garbage bags drop as he threw them at me, even though they were disgusting and I became disgusting for touching them. *Just a few more weeks and I'm home.*

Giddu told me to fill one cart at a time until it filled. He waited for me as I wheeled the barrow into his home and emptied it out on the floor of his living room, separated from the kitchen by absolutely nothing. When I came back a half minute later, he had already finished filling half of the second barrow. I emptied out all our garbage on giddu's dirty tiled floors in a few minutes.

"Now for the best part," giddu said as he made his way off the back of his truck. "The sorting."

Sorting? I had awoke at two in the morning, brushed my teeth in the company of roaches in a free man's prison cell, endured giddu's victory rant about finding a ring in a bag of garbage, and barrowed my way through a building for a good hour and a half. Asking me to bury my hands in the garbage – I just didn't have it in me. Not then at least.

"Can I go for a walk for a bit?" I asked.

"Do it after," he said. "We have a lot of garbage to get through."

"I'm just gonna do it now," I said as I waved goodbye and walked away. "So I can watch the sunrise. I'll be back later to help though."

I staggered through the dust as I walked away and wished I didn't need to lie to giddu to get out from spending time with him. In a way, I admired his simplicity. I'd never met a man so proud of his own dirt. Or maybe it wasn't pride. Maybe he didn't understand his position in society. I doubt he'd never heard the jokes, never heard the term zabal, garbage man, as an insult. I thought back to the Virgin, smiling at the people like they were no different from everyone else. I just couldn't get it.

Still, I hoped he'd be done when I came back.

"Suit yourself," he said shaking his head. "But try to be here before breakfast. I've got a special surprise for you."

I nodded, though I already knew what the surprise was. Yesterday, my mom told me she'd be back the next morning with breakfast from McDonalds. She told me she never ate at any foreign restaurants when she lived with giddu because there were none in Moqattam when she was young. I doubted there were any now. This could've been my grandpa's first time eating American food.

I trekked towards the mountains through the sandy streets, kicked through the plastic bags and bottles and tried my way around the compost heaps. I passed a few boys and girls around my age wading through the trash, separating bottles from papers from the rest. An old woman with her hair tied and loosely covered by a black veil sat helping them.

One of the bigger boys picked up an empty plastic Fanta bottle and tossed it at his younger sister's head. She shrieked and cursed his hand and ran at him.

"I was testing your reflexes," he laughed as he blocked her open palm.

A little boy, maybe three years old, sitting on a clear plastic bag and naked from the waist down (except for a pair of black socks) cried at the sight. The old woman shook her head and picked the boy up and kissed him on his forehead, his bare bottom facing me, and scolded the older kids. She carried him over to the pile of garbage, sat him on her lap and gave him a bottle to play with. He whipped it back at the pile, laughed, and reached for another. His arms were too small to grab hold of anything, and his mother wouldn't give him another after that. *He spared himself the garbage* I thought. He was better off. But still, he cried for that bottle.

Looking at the child on my side, I didn't notice the already separated pile of bottles in front of me as I walked into them.

The whole heap collapsed. I looked forward, stepped back and watched the bottles roll away from their mound.

"What are you doing?" a small voice cried from behind the broken pile. I looked down and saw a small brown girl in a little yellow poncho and a beige toque covering her head. It was a cold dawn.

She looked maybe seven, skinny with a clenched fist the size of an egg. The other held a bottle it couldn't grasp for long. Not in a hand that small. She had real fat cheeks like a squirrel storing food in its mouth.

"Sorry," I said. "I didn't see where I was walking."

"Yes you did," she said scratching her head with her closed fist. She threw the bottle in her hand onto the pile. "Look how big the pile is. An elephant could see it."

"No I didn't – "

"You come on my land and try to steal my garbage fatty?" she stomped her foot like she was trying to scare away a fly.

"No!" I yelled.

"I know how you fatties work," she said as she walked towards me and picked up all the bottles on her way, throwing them back on the pile. "You take all our good garbage and eat all our money like pigs."

Pigs?

Surprisingly, I wasn't angry. I felt sorry for her if anything. She needed a sandwich.

"I don't want your bottles," I said.

"Yes you do, you fat."

"I don't want your bottles or any of your money. I walked into your bottles accidentally. I'm sorry."

She let go of the bottles on the floor, stood up and straightened her poncho. She examined my face with her wide brown eyes. I examined hers. Her eyes made her way down to my old Reeboks, then back up at my face.

"You're a liar," she said flatly. "A fat liar."

She turned away from me and towards her stash, reached down to the floor and picked up her bottles. She took an armful, held them towards her heart like she was carrying a baby, and threw them in a bag beside the load, one by one. She was a tiny transporter, quick and efficient and stopped for nothing. She strode from bottle to plastic bag like a veteran.

I looked down to her feet. She wasn't wearing shoes. Her tiny feet looked sooty and dry. I almost wanted them to be clean. I almost wanted to hose them down and watch the dirt wash off her toes and down to the soil where it belonged. But that wasn't for me to do. Washing a little girl's feet is a mother's job.

"Where's your mother?" I asked.

She turned her head around towards me as she tied up her first bag full of bottles.

"I don't talk to fatty liars," she said tightening the knot.

She stared at me, her eyes narrow and heavy, full of something I knew but couldn't name. Something like hunger, but she didn't look like she wanted to eat. Although she needed to. She was hungry for something I knew I needed too.

She picked up another plastic bag and waved it in the light breeze until it was full of air. She held it in her left hand and reached down for a bottle with her right. I picked up a bottle beside me, making sure the girl noticed. I walked towards her.

"I'm putting it in," I said.

She stared at me for a moment, turned towards the bottles, there were so many, and back up on me. She opened the mouth of the bag. I threw the bottle in and reached for another.

The little girl watched me pick up bottle after bottle and throw it in the bag. After a while, she moved from her spot and followed me around as I picked them up. She had a funny shuffle to her quiet steps, keeping her feet close to the ground as she walked.

"Mama's cooking breakfast for baba right now," she said. "He should be back from his garbage run soon, if he isn't already."

"Oh," I said nodding. "Do they know you're out separating bottles?"

"Yes."

"Do they know you're not wearing any shoes?"

"I learned this from baba," she said. "Shoes are uncomfortable in the heat."

She was right, though it wasn't hot just yet. But during the midday, my feet felt hot and moist, like they were being gently poached.

"I think you need to wash your feet."

"I washed them last night. I wash them every night. They just keep getting dirty."

"Well why don't you wear sandals?"

"This feels nicer," she smiled wriggling her tiny toes. "The fat one is the boss."

"Your little Goliath?" I said. I always thought big toes were too big and useless. They didn't deserve the power they had over all the smaller guys.

We were down to the last bottle after a few minutes. I threw it in and she tied it up. She had three garbage bags full of bottles that morning. The little girl looked at them and smiled. A job well done. She took off her toque and hung it from her waistband beneath her poncho. She turned to look at me, then back to the bottles.

"It was a lot faster with another person," she said.

"Yes it was."

She nodded. The girl walked over to the bag she'd just tied, untied it, and pulled out a large plastic Miranda Orange bottle. She tied the bag back up.

"You can have this one."

"I don't want your garbage," I said, waving no with my hand.

The girl shuffled towards me and forced the bottle between my arm and side of my stomach.

"There you go," she said. "You go now. I'm gonna do the cans myself."

"Okay," I said, a little irritated. I really didn't want her bottle.

"Thank you."

I walked away towards giddu. I still didn't want to help him separate his garbage, but I felt I owed it to him since I helped a little garbage girl I didn't know and not my own grandpa. I marched slowly, wondering how many times a girl that small could wash her feet in the few years she'd lived.

A girl as thin as her could compete in Little Miss pageants in Canada if she wasn't so dirty. And those fat cheeks, like she hid something in her mouth she didn't want anyone to see. Nobody was around her to see it anyway. Maybe that's what she was hiding. She was all alone.

I spotted giddu as I approached him. He wasn't working, just sitting outside smoking shisha and admiring his Chevy. I waved and he waved back.

"Oh good news," he beamed and puffed as I approached.

I held the bottle the little girl gave me out towards him. He smiled and threw up a hand in victory.

"Even more good news," he yelled triumphantly. He grabbed it from me and examined it, turned it widthwise in his hand.

"The Lord gives," he said as he set it down beside him.

I took a seat next to him and watched him smoke.

"I thought you were supposed to be separating your garbage?" I said.

"A man can't rest?" he yelled with a flat palm facing the sky.

Fair enough. I turned towards his Chevy, now dirty after our short trip to Cairo.

"I think you like it," he said as he stared along with me.

"It's nice," I lied.

"Nice?" he winced. "It's more beautiful today than the first day I got it. Big and strong, like you. I feel like a boss when I'm driving it."

I nodded and thought back to that girl's fat toe. But unlike her Goliath, I knew his Chevy wasn't useless. He'd have no money without it.

"This truck is my America," he said, shaking his head agreeing with his own words. He looked at me and took a puff of his shisha, blowing the smoke out of his nose like Truckasaurus. It was a lot easier to be a boss when you lived in a community of garbage pickers. He was happy. Maybe if I'd lived here long enough, I would be too.

"Yeah. So when are we gonna get to work?" Might as well get it over with I thought.

"In a while my friend. Don't worry." He crossed his legs and turned towards the road out of Moqattam. "I'm just waiting for someone right now. I got a big surprise for you coming real soon my friend. Huge."

HER NAME IS EGYPT

In the heat of thousands of marching bodies, under the tinted grey of downtown Cairo's smoggy sky, Botros rode on his big brother Ramy's shoulders towards Tahrir. Everyone looked tired to Botros, but no one acted tired.

Most of the people around Botros were men, clean cut and in their twenties, around Ramy's age. There were a few girls here and there. Some with their heads covered, some without.

Botros held his head high above the crowd. He watched them cry "Freedom!" and "Get out!" as they pumped their fists and waved Egyptian flags in the air.

So this is what they called Revolution. Maybe if everyone yelled loud enough, the President would finally hear them.

"Silence was our disease," one man yelled, skinny and bearded with rotting yellow teeth. "We are cured! We are cured!"

Ramy picked his little brother up off his shoulders and lowered Botros to where he could whisper in his ear.

"You see that man?" he whispered in Botros' ear. "That man's an idiot."

Botros nodded and Ramy threw him back up onto his shoulders. Botros watched the yellow toothed man run through the crowd. *We are cured!* he cried with that sense of stupid hope Botros had only ever seen in Egyptian dramas. Botros didn't know what the yellow toothed man was there for, but he wished he could talk to him. He wished he could tell him about his sister Mariam. She was nine, two years older than him.

Wide dark eyes and honey-brown skin, thick black curly locks, she looked almost identical to her baby brother. She wasn't fat like him though, and she let him know it. She used to tell him he looked like an eggplant from his head to his thighs and laugh and laugh and he'd throw something at her head and she'd bob out of the way and laugh even harder. He didn't know why she liked hating him so much. It only ever happened when he got any attention.

One time she caught him listening to Amr Diab in the kitchen with Ramy who he'd asked to teach him to dance. He barely started to shake his hips before a clementine hit him on the side of his head. "Eggplants are only good for cooking," she smiled, her eyes wanting what she knew was coming. She laughed and Ramy laughed and Amr Diab crooned in the background of the woman he once loved and had gone away. Botros chased her down the short hall and she screamed, though he knew she wasn't scared of him. He hated running, but she loved being chased. And he never caught her.

But one day he would, and he'd show her what he needed to show her. The day was coming. She'd started slowing down recently, complaining of headaches every so often. Her mother gave her Tylenol. She usually got better pretty soon. But he'd have his chance.

Two weeks ago, he'd gotten a hat as a gift from his cousins visiting from Canada on their last day in the country. He loved it. It was a black Toronto Blue Jays baseball cap, too big for his small head, but it fit Mariam just fine. He promised his cousins he'd wear it to school every day. He never made it that far. Mariam snatched it off his head every morning and made him chase her to school, a few minutes from their apartment. He knew what was coming. He tried to fight her off in the mornings, holding his hat to his head or hugging it to his chest as he walked beside her. She waited until he relaxed his grip, he always did, and plucked it off him.

But finally, just a few days before the Revolution, on a hot Sunday morning, Mariam didn't touch the cap on his head. Botros was so happy, he'd finally get a chance to show all his friends the hat his cousins bought him.

"*Blue Jays*," he'd tell his friends. "It's a team named after a bird. Mariam used to steal it from me in the morning but I grew too strong for her."

He hadn't grown stronger. Mariam had gotten weaker. She walked him to school that morning, her gaze lowered to the cracks in the pavement. She looked like she was tired, she needed to sit.

"What's wrong with you today?" Botros said. "You look stupid like that."

"My head hurts," she said. "Everything's so loud." He watched her cover her ears and cringe. Tears rolled down her cheeks. This didn't seem like her usual headaches. It looked a lot worse.

"You cry like a girl," he said. She stopped at a garbage can and held on to its side. She wiped the tears from her eyes and breathed a light breath. Botros tried to hear what she heard. Engines and horns, a light wind, drivers cursing at each other from their open windows – it was no different than any other morning. She probably had just eaten some bad meat. It wouldn't have been the first time.

Two minutes later, she let go of the rim of the garbage can and walked behind Botros, her head still facing the floor. He told her to hurry. She almost always held his hand and pulled him forward when she wasn't being chased, she needed him to know who led and who followed, but today she lagged behind. The boy felt freedom well within him, like an island at high tide.

She dropped him off at his school and walked across the street on her own. He wasn't fazed. He showed his friends all the different ways kids wore their hats in Canada, the ways his cousins showed him.

She didn't walk home with him that day. Ramy picked him up.

"Where's Mariam?" Botros asked.

"She's in the hospital," Ramy said.

"Why?"

Ramy turned his head towards the passing cars for a moment, then back to the road.

"She's got a bad tooth," Ramy said.

"Did they fix it?"

"Not yet."

"Why not?"

"You have some money you could lend me to pay for her surgery?" he yelled throwing his palm up to Botros. Botros pushed his brother's hand away.

"You could sell your car."

"This piece of garbage?" Ramy said peeling a piece of tape off the side of Botros' seat. "I'd have to pay someone to take it."

Botros nodded and played with the tape, tearing it off completely.

"Ask Uncle Sami, Canadians have too much money," he said, sticking the tape back onto the tear.

Ramy nodded and let his shoulders loose. Botros heard his breathing slow. Ramy ran a hand down through his hair.

"Maybe," he said.

They took her home a few nights later, her face now pale and tired. Their mother made her hot lemonade at dinner time, since she refused to eat, and strapped a small wooden frame with a picture of St. Demiana around Mariam's head using a church headscarf. She put her hand on Mariam's head and mumbled something to Jesus. She left a few minutes later, she still hadn't made dinner for Botros' dad who'd be home in an hour.

Mariam had a fever now and could barely talk, though she listened. His mother told him to go and talk to his sister. She needed someone and Ramy was at work.

"I don't want to talk to her," he said. "She'll throw something at me."

His mother slammed the knife in her hand on the counter and jerked him towards her by his shirt. She held him in front of her, her cold wet hands gripping the back of his neck, and stared him in his eyes. Her brow raised like she wanted to be angry. He knew she wasn't angry. Her eyes were wet. She was tired.

"Do you want baba to find out?" she whispered. He shrugged her off and walked to his sister's room.

"Remember, she can't talk," his mother said just loud enough for him to hear. He knew that already. Her tooth hurt.

He sat at the edge of her bed, hat off, trying to think of what to say. She stared at him, heavy eyed and pale and smiling, as if on some opiate. She wasn't on any opiate.

Botros couldn't think of anything to say, so he told her a story she knew well. Botros knew she loved listening to stories about herself, maybe even more than living them.

"Remember last Easter in Alexandria? We were walking down the Nile to tayta and giddu's home, and we heard a loud snatch sound like kshhhhh and we looked at the water bank and there was an alligator!" She smiled and nodded. She knew what was coming.

"And you said we needed to get it to go away somehow or it'd eat us, so I yelled 'go away you stupid alligator or we'll eat you!' but it just stayed. So you picked up a rock and threw it at him and we ran away?"

She shook her head yes.

"I need to find that alligator again," he said. "I think it ate my watch. Remember my *Ninja Turtles* watch?"

Mariam giggled, then winced and rested her head on her pillow. Something in her laugh hurt her. Botros felt it, but he couldn't name it. She waved him towards her. He crawled onto the bed. Mariam licked her lips open.

"Water," she whispered. "Cold."

Botros nodded a quick nod and ran towards the kitchen. He fetched a cold glass of water and brought it back to her. She smiled, took the glass from him and drank.

She finished her water and tried to open her mouth again.

"Don't talk anymore!" he yelled.

"Thankou," she said, squinting. She turned her head, and fell asleep.

She laid in her bed, the lights on, mouth closed, still as the night. He could only hear her breathe, and he wondered if she was still his sister. He never felt so big. Or, she never looked so small.

Everything, their home and the room they shared and the clanking of pots from the kitchen felt so quiet, dissociated from a world that now lived outside their room. In his newly acquired peace, Botros realized he missed her.

"I'm going to Tahrir in the morning," Ramy told his little brother. "To make Mubarak pay for her tooth." Ramy laughed at himself a moment later, mumbling something about being an idiot for trying to believe that garbage.

Botros hated when Ramy second guessed himself. In Botros' mind, this was all he could do. Walk and yell "Freedom!" and ask the government to fix his sister's tooth. He dreamed of meeting the President himself, telling him Mariam's story. The President cared in his dreams. If only he could get to him. Ramy left his parents a note in the kitchen, and took Botros in the early morning to Tahrir.

~~~

Botros rode on his brother's shoulders for half an hour until they reached Tahrir. A group of teenagers were stationed in front of the Square checking ID cards at a steel barricade. One man, tall and skinny with a thin moustache, stood in front of the barricade, each arm tied to one of the railings.

"What'd he do?" Ramy asked pointing to the man.

"His ID said he was police, so we're giving him the royal treatment," a teen said. "Isn't that right Mr. Police Man, sir?" The tied man didn't answer. The teenager laughed.

"Good morning Captain," Ramy said and smiled and gave a shallow bow as he passed the officer.

Botros rode on his brother's shoulders the rest of the way to Tahrir. He spotted a small tent city in the heart of the Square. "We're here!" he yelled. Ramy took him off his shoulders and plopped him on the ground. He grabbed the boy's hand and walked towards the protesters circling Tahrir. A short, skinny man with the fat face of a cow and the bark of a dog rode on his people's shoulders singing slogans he read off a sheet of paper. "Leave means leave! We've made our stand," he chanted, punching his chest. "Take your pride, leave us our land." The protesters sang and many banged their chests after him.

"Captain," a woman's voice sang behind Botros. The boy noticed the voice right away. He smiled and turned around. There was Engi. Green eyes and brown hair and soft skin Engi. The kind Botros saw on television in soap commercials. He had all but cried when he found out Ramy was soon to be engaged to her. She smiled, her mouth and her eyes, and picked him up and kissed him on his forehead and called him her little prince. "If only you were my age," she said, "I'd leave your brother in a heartbeat." Botros pointed to his cheek. She kissed him again on his cheek and ran her hand through his hard, black hair. Up close, her hair smelled like green apple.

She smiled at him for a moment, though her eyes grew tender, sweet. Maybe sad. "What a handsome little prince," she said. "My friend Samia's here with her baby. Wanna go talk to her? You can meet her daughter." Botros nodded and she dropped him back down, held his hand, and led him to a sidewalk in Tahrir.

He could feel her turn to him every now and then as they walked. He felt the gravity of her eyes, they were so heavy.

"Did you tell him yet?" she whispered to Ramy.

"Shh," he whispered back.

Botros looked up at the two of them.

"Tell me what?" he asked.

Ramy looked down at Botros, sighed, and looked back up.

"You wanna know?" he asked.

"Yes."

"Are you sure? I don't think you'll like it."

"Tell me!"

"Here it goes," he breathed. "You're getting a little too fat."

"No I'm not! I'm handsome. Even Engi thinks I'm handsome."

Engi laughed, though she sounded nervous, and patted the boy's head. "More handsome than your brother at least," she said. Ramy nudged her.

"I'm joking," she said. "You're not so bad either." Botros smiled.

"There she is," Engi said, pointing at a young woman sitting on a beach chair outside a closed café in Tahrir. "Her daughter's name is Aida, she's five."

Samia stood up when she saw them. She shook Ramy's hand and kissed Engi on each cheek. She turned to Botros. "So this is the little prince?" she said. "Engi pointed you out to me when she saw you from far away."

She was a chunky girl, heavy thighs, fat cheeks and an honest smile. Her daughter, who sat on another beach chair with her head rested on her palm, eyes closed in the heat and noise, looked exactly like her. All except the hair, which was much softer than her mother's.

"Ramy and I have to discuss something for a minute. Botros, can you take care of Samia for a while? She gets lonely."

"Yes I can," he said. Samia laughed. Ramy and Engi waved goodbye and walked towards the Square.

"Sit," Samia said, picking Aida up from her seat and placing her on her lap. Aida didn't fuss. She rested her head against her mother's chest and closed her eyes again.

"She's really tired," Samia said. "She didn't sleep much last night. We camped out right there," she pointed at the tents in the middle of Tahrir. "It was a long night."

Botros climbed onto the beach chair.

"She's so small," he said. "Does she know how to dance?"

Samia smiled.

"She did some dancing last night."

Botros wondered how much money he'd need to buy Aida as a wife. He knew he couldn't ask Ramy for help. Ramy still couldn't afford to pay for his own engagement. Botros wondered how he would pay for Aida if he wanted to marry her. He couldn't think of anything. But he loved the idea of a tiny dancer wife. Still, she was no Engi. Engi called him her little prince. She sang to him and bought him little cheese balls wrapped in red plastic. He never liked cheese before she first bought him some. There was only one Engi.

"Do you dance?" Samia asked.

"I love to dance. I have an Amr Diab CD at home and Ramy taught me to dance."

"Oh ya?" Samia giggled. "Can you show me?"

"It's easy," he said as he stood up. He threw his hands to his sides and started to shake his hips to a beat he heard in his head. Samia laughed and clapped on beat to his sway. She threw a flat palm above her lips and ululated, then clapped again. A smiling man with a tabla approached him as he danced, rested against the wall with the tabla between his feet, and played his drum to the boy's rhythm. A few young people, men and women, who were passing by saw the young boy dancing to the tabla. Their laughter turned to clapping which turned to dancing for many. As the crowd grew, Botros became frustrated. All his life, Mariam never let him steal any of her parent's attention. He finally had a moment others watched and clapped and cheered for him, and it was hijacked by teenagers. Botros stopped dancing and walked back to his seat.

"Look what you started," Samia smiled. The dancing girls and boys and the ululating women and the man playing tabla went on without him just a few feet from where he sat. "You're not a little prince, you're a Casanova."

"What's that?"

"You'll find out eventually."

Botros nodded and set his stare on Aida again.

"Why don't you let her sleep in the tent?"

"It's too hot in the tent in the day. But I might leave soon anyways. I think she might be getting sick."

Botros sat back in his seat and examined the little girl's face. Her mouth was open. One of her ears was red, though that could've been because of the heat. She snored, very quietly.

"She doesn't look sick."

"I hope not."

"My sister Mariam is sick."

Samia frowned and nodded.

"I heard. I'm very sorry."

"That's okay. We just need to get her surgery to replace her dead tooth."

"Dead tooth?"

"Yeah. Didn't Ramy tell you?"

Samia furrowed her brow. "Oh, yeah," she said. "I guess he did. Yeah he told me about the dead tooth."

"He and my dad are working to make some money and soon she'll be alright. I'm hoping to find Mubarak to see if he can help me."

Samia looked away towards the crowd and examined them. She bit her lower lip, chewing her words before they escaped. Botros wanted to tell her to say what she thought, but he couldn't. He knew she probably wouldn't. She turned back to Botros and nodded. Her air lightened, now hopeful. For a moment, her round face shone like the moon.

"Your sister," she said, "is Egypt."

"Her name is Mariam."

"Her name is Egypt," she said. "Maybe we just need to pull out the old tooth."

"Egypt doesn't even have teeth to need a new one."

"Let's hope that's all it needs."

Botros leaned against the nylon backrest of his beach chair. He suddenly felt heavy, anchored to the bottom of his seat. He felt the world rotating underneath him. The sky stood still. Everything around him felt like nothing more than a moving picture, a horribly dull movie he was forced to watch. Everybody sang and laughed and clapped and danced and protested and cursed and spat, but Mariam was still sick.

Last night, he'd seen his father at the dinner table, his head lowered to the empty plate in front of him, his eyes bloodshot. Botros' mother had wept as she'd served her husband dinner and told him to pray and pleaded the Virgin's intercession.

"She'll grow and get educated. She'll become a doctor someday, God willing. And we'll find her a nice man and she'll get married," his mother said. His father waited until he was composed before he went on night watch with a few of his neighbours now that there were no police to protect their property from being looted. Every man had a post.

"Where's your husband?" Botros asked Samia.

"I dunno. He could be with another woman now for all I know."

"You don't see him anymore?"

"We're divorced. I think he's in Saudi right now. You wanna eat?" she asked. He nodded. Samia pulled out a cucumber from her purse. She broke off a piece and passed it to Botros.

The last Saudi Botros had seen was on the night of Easter Sunday. His father took the whole family out to Montazah Beach in Alexandria. They ate at a Chinese all you can eat restaurant that Botros knew probably cost his dad a fortune. He probably emptied most of his funds on that small vacation. Ramy told him not to do it because they may need it in the future.

"You only live once," Botros' dad said. "Maybe if you'd gave up some of your pride, I could have leant you the money and you'd be engaged by now."

Ramy ignored his father's words.

Everyone that sat around Botros in the Chinese restaurant looked rich. White businessmen in black suits and striped ties, a few white women in warm coloured pantsuits. Even a table of Asians. Soft black hair, narrow slanted eyes – they, along with the Asian staff, looked just like how Botros had seen them on television. Though they weren't as short as he imagined them.

A man in a white galabeya sat across from Botros' table and hovered above a plate of food. He ate slowly. He was a dark man, darker than Botros, with sparse facial hair he permed into a tidy goatee. A red and white kuffeya rested on his hair, held together by a thick black band that tied it around the crown of his head. His eyes were dark, hostile, though his brows looked plucked. He sat infront of Botros' table and stared right through him and his family, who sat by the window in front of the pier. The man watched the passing boats as he ate.

"We have a Saudi in the house," Botros' father whispered to Mariam. "Everybody watch your wallets." Everyone at the table laughed, though no one turned to look at the Saudi to draw attention to their making fun of him.

Botros ate as much as he could trying to clear out the restaurant on his father's orders. "Let them know they made a huge mistake letting us into an all you can eat restaurant," he told them. Mariam stopped at two plates. Botros and his mother stopped at three and waited for Ramy and his father to finish. They were both on their fifth plates. Botros' stomach hurt. He had eaten too much and the smell of food around him made him sick. With half-closed eyes, he watched the Saudi as he finished his food. The Saudi threw his head back from a small burp, pushed his plate in front of him, and took out a cigarette and lit it.

The Asian staff stared at him and yelled amongst themselves in a language Botros couldn't understand. A middle-aged waiter nodded at his staff and walked towards the Saudi.

"Sir," he said, "This family restaurant. You in no smoke zone. You want smoke, walk to smoke zone," he pointed at the other side of the restaurant.

The Saudi stared him in his eyes for a long, long moment, with the cigarette between his fingers. He put the cigarette in his mouth, looked away from the Asian towards the boats, and took a drag.

"Sir, big fine sir. You smoke in no smoke zone, big fine."

The Saudi leaned forward with the cigarette in his mouth. "How much?"

"Five thousand pound sir. Big fine."

The Saudi pulled a suitcase from underneath him, opened it on his lap, pulled out the cash and rested it on the table in five small stacks, then mounted them into one. The Asian looked at it, picked it up, counted it. He nodded, "Thank you sir," and walked away.

Everyone in the restaurant saw it. Botros' father stopped eating, stared at the Saudi, then put the spoon to his face and ate even faster. Everyone except Botros, who was too sick to process what had happened, sat in awe. Mariam turned to her father.

"Baba," she whispered, "is he a monster?"

"Yes Marmar," he whispered back. "He is."

Botros vomited on the bus home that night. His father slapped him on the backside of his head. "You threw up my money," he said. Botros couldn't tell if he was joking.

"I don't like Saudi's," Botros told Samia. "If your husband is with a Saudi woman, he deserves to be with a Saudi woman."

Samia laughed. Her daughter dug her face into her mother's chest. Botros heard a wave of screams swell behind him. From the corner of his eyes, he saw Ramy and Engi jog back. They looked scared.

"We need to go," Ramy said. "The Mubarak thugs are here."

Botros looked behind him. He saw stones fly and heard them plink against the tanks that rolled between the two sides of feuding protesters. Botros saw a ball of fire fly through the air over the tanks and onto the anti-government protesters that had their backs against him. He watched many of them turn towards him and run away from the flying stones and Molotov cocktails and burning bags of garbage. One man was hit with a cocktail and fell to the ground.

"Have mercy on me Allah!" he screamed over and over until the frightened crowd caught up to him. Botros heard a sharp crack as the crowd ran onto his back. The man stopped screaming. The crowd motioned around the man as the flames grew, keeping their distance from the blaze. The fire on his back spread throughout his body and he lay still, facing the ground, being eaten by flames.

"We need to go," Ramy yelled. Samia stood and ran with Aida in her arms, she'd just woken up and started to cry. Samia never waved goodbye.

"What about that man on fire?" Botros asked.

"Get up!" Ramy and Engi yelled, over and over.

"What about Mariam?" he asked. He heard the patter of hooves drum against asphalt. The sound grew louder as something approached. Ramy turned around.

A band of men on brown horses and one with a red towel wrapped around his head riding a camel stampeded towards them. All of them held long wooden sticks they used to whip the protesters as they passed, crying *God is great!* Ramy picked the boy up into his arms and ran in the direction of the crowd with Engi at his side. Botros watched the pro-Mubarak protesters ride down the streets behind them, they were fast approaching, and cried.

"What about Mariam," he yelled, "We didn't talk to the President yet."

Engi and Ramy kept running. Ramy threw his brother over the barricades and off the streets before the riders could get to him. He helped Engi over, then jumped over himself. Botros watched a few men catch up to a rider in a green shirt from behind. They grabbed his shirt and threw him off his horse which trotted away without him. The protesters kicked him in his gut and punched him in his face and the back of his head until he bled.

"I didn't mean to hurt you," he cried in a half-daze as they beat him, his head dangling against his torso. Some anti-Mubarak protesters tried to stop others from beating on the man, while others pushed them aside and swung at the back of his neck. The man bled from the side of his head as he was carried away, half dead.

This man worked for the President. That meant the President didn't want to talk to Botros. He didn't care about his sister or her tooth or anything. A strange feeling welled up within Botros' gut. He didn't know if he was disgusted or just sick, but he did want to see everything destroyed. Like the man hit by the Molotov cocktail, he wanted Tahrir to burn.

"Kill him!" he cried, punching against Ramy's back as Ramy ran. "Kill him! Break his tooth!"

Ramy pushed through the crowds, Engi running in front of him and clearing the way. They arrived at their car twenty minutes later. Engi called the friend who'd driven her to Tahrir that morning to tell her she would go home with Ramy. Botros sat in the front beside his brother, Engi in the back.

"You took us to Tahrir for nothing!" Botros yelled at his brother. "How are we gonna get the money now? How is she gonna get better?"

"What do you know about money?" Ramy yelled back. "Are you gonna pay for her? Are ou gonna go out and work sixteen hours a day to make enough money to buy a few tomatoes and fish for the night?"

"Why aren't you smoking in restaurants yet? What's wrong with you? When I'm your age, I'll own twelve Asians! Twelve!"

Ramy bit his lip. His face flushed hot red. His right eyebrow raised and held. "What's a matter with me?" he punched his dashboard. "What's a matter with me? You're sitting here dreaming of owning a bunch of Chinese slaves and smoking in restaurants like some filthy Saudi while your sister's at home with a tumour the size of your fist in her brain – dying – you understand that word? Dying? You still want to know what's a matter with me? Do you want me to paint you a picture of a grave next to bunnies and pretty pretty flowers?"

Botros went quiet. He felt Engi's stare from behind him, once gentle, now pitiful. He felt the midday sun beat down on his eyes. He blocked it with the backend of his hand above his brow. Rows of palm trees passed by him, one by one. For a moment, he sat back in that Chinese restaurant in Alexandria, staring at the Saudi and wanting to throw up.

"She's dying?" he asked.

Ramy didn't answer right away. Botros knew he was thinking. He always second guessed himself.

"No. I got angry. I made some things up to scare you. I'm sorry."

Yes. He was angry. He turned into a monster for a moment and lied because he was angry. Ugly lies. What an ugly liar.

Mariam had a dead tooth. She, herself, was not dying. Impossible. She was nine years old, two years older than him. Botros didn't ask any more questions. He kept quiet for the rest of the car ride, and watched the palm trees pass him by, one by one.

But in his mind, he remembered all the things Mariam said to him over the years. All the times she taunted him, called him fat, stole his hat. All the things she'd done and he could do nothing to stop her. His anger built upon itself as he piled up her sins against him. When he got home, he'd tell her. He'd finally have the chance to tell her.

They got to their apartment a few minutes after Ramy dropped off Engi. Botros marched straight to Mariam's room while Ramy went to say hello to his mother who was cooking in the kitchen. He slammed the door open. Mariam sat with her back against three pillows piled on top of each other, facing upwards. Still pale, she'd lost a lot of weight on her body. Her cheeks stripped to the bone of fat. She looked the same that morning, but he never noticed her cheekbones before.

But her eyes, still wide. Still brown. But tired. So tired.

She saw him and smiled. Botros felt something empty him from the inside, like his big sister cut out his entrails with a knife. He no longer wanted to vomit and he couldn't remember all the things he planned on saying to her. He softened as she readjusted his insides with her stare. She waved him towards her and he walked without thinking, in a half-trance. She turned her face towards the wall, cautiously fishing for something behind her pillow. She turned back around, and pulled out a plastic, green Teenage Mutant Ninja Turtles watch.

"I foun it," she hushed, "behine my pillow. I was hiding it from you." Botros stood there, he lowered his gaze to the ground. He was scared to look up and see her face again. She took his wrist and pulled him towards her and kissed him on his cheek.

He sat down on the side of the bed, dangling his feet above the bare concrete floor. He took his hat off, the one his cousins gave him, held it in his right hand. Watched his feet dangle above the concrete. He turned to Mariam who sat smiling, always smiling. Such tired eyes. He got on his knees on the bed and leaned his left side on the bed post. He reached for her face, held his thumb to her forehead with his left hand. Her face was hot. With his right hand, he took his hat, placed it on her head, and sat back on the bed.

"It fits your head better," he said, and laid down next to her, trying to think of a story she'd want to hear.

All the memories that worked into his mind were painful to think about. Everything he once hated, he now missed.

"Remember that time you threw a clementine at my head?"

He felt her smile and nod and knew she wanted to hear it, although he didn't want to say it because he knew how it ended.

FIRST CRUSADE

A skinned cow hock strung from a hook in front of a butcher shop dangled in front of Demiana. From the backseat of the old Peugeot, she watched the hock sway gently with the wind.

Zainab sat in front of Demiana. Demiana knew she hated the smell too. But Zainab's father who sat behind the wheel didn't seem to mind. *All he's probably ever known is cow hock* Demiana thought. He drove them past a half dozen butcher shops every morning on the ten minute drive to their school.

The light turned green and Zainab's father drove off. They stopped on the side of the street in front of the all girl's school after a few blocks. Demiana stepped out from the car towards the front passenger's side and opened the door for Zainab who sat adjusting her headscarf. Demiana waved goodbye to Zainab's father. He nodded and patted his chest twice in recognition without turning to look at her, and drove off.

Demiana walked with Zainab, shoulder to shoulder, towards their school that sat under the floating sun. Sometimes Demiana felt like closing her eyes and walking towards the sun instead, if there was only a staircase that could extend upwards into the sky. She'd open her eyes once she climbed high enough, to see every crater and mound and crevice as she imagined it. To see the sun as a whole. She'd only ever known it from so far.

The school was a small beige chalet that stood on a bed of

sanded rocks in front of a forest of palm trees that stretched towards the pale blue sky. An Egyptian flag hung from a pole in the middle of the courtyard, gently fluttering with the weak wind in front of the lone pillar on the northern end of the school. The two girls saw their classmates, some of them sitting on the uneven alabaster ledge, some standing in front of the dome-cut mirrors or the closed wooden doors of the portico. All of them were talking and laughing, all of them between the tenth and twelfth grade, in blue vest-white shirt-blue dress pant uniforms. Half of them in headscarves.

But Demiana was different. She was one of a handful of Nazarenes in her high school, and like a few others, wore a cross outside her school uniform. A few girls in her school looked at her like she was an alien, though they tried not to show it.

The cross used to belong to Sara, Demiana's older sister. Demiana had seen it around Sara's neck ever since she could remember. On the day of her engagement, Sara found Demiana studying in the room they shared for sixteen years, and sat next to her on the bed. She took the cross off from around her neck.

"You're the oldest girl after I'm gone," she said as she put the cross around Demiana. "It's your turn now. ou need to learn to cook."

Cook? Demiana thought. She boiled eggs and pounded dough for bread all the time. Sometimes she even fried meat for the family when her mother and older sister were busy. She knew how to cook. But she was terrified of this cross that now hung around her neck, an anchor that weighed her to something she belonged to but didn't understand.

Demiana pinched the ends of her sleeves and rolled the fabric between her fingers. She stared at a spot on the floor behind Sara and bit at her bottom lip.

"You're doing it again," Sara said.

"Doing what?"

"Pinching your sleeves."

"No I'm not."

"You don't need to be nervous. Growing old is good, you'll learn a lot about the world," Sara said and patted the cross against Demiana's chest, "and about who you are."

She already knew who she was. Demiana Makram Ibrahim Fanoos Abdel-Messih. She loved Soad Hosny movies and pretty much every song by Umm Kalthoum, except *A Thousand and One Nights* (it just dragged on). She was the youngest of two daughters and four brothers. All the rest were married, except Sara who was engaged. The cross didn't make her into something. She already existed.

"Get ready for church," Sara told her, throwing a white dress shirt at Demiana. "I'll see you downstairs in five minutes." Demiana snuck her cross beneath her dress shirt.

She went to church with her sister every week because she was expected to. She covered her head with a scarf and sat on the women's side with Sara and watched an old bearded man with a funny black hat and a large metal crucific around his neck wave a golden censer around the altar, muttering prayers in Arabic and Coptic. Sara understood Coptic, but Demiana never bothered to learn. Many of Demiana's church friends urged her to come to Coptic class. She went through so many excuses. She was just lazy. She sat through sermons, but she didn't listen. Sometimes, she slept. But that day, she couldn't sleep.

Church was no different than every other Friday afternoon service. She sat there, her new cross tucked behind the buttons of her dress shirt, and watched the old priest wave his censer and pray words she didn't understand, though she was too nervous to be bored. She realized Sara was leaving. She needed to listen. Maybe the priest knew what was coming.

The sermon that night was on obedience in a time of Passover.

"They were slaves," the priest spoke with a quiet intensity. "The pyramids you see in Giza were the work of their hands. They were strangers in a strange land, this Egypt." The priest explained the years of slavery and oppression, the sting of the whips of the Egyptians who owned the land. He talked of God's love and Moses' mercy for his people. The signs, the wonders, and the plagues, that led up to the Passover, when the first born of every Egyptian was taken in the night.

"With the sign of the blood of lambs, the Hebrews were spared and saved. Even under the scornful eye of the Egyptians, that saw their doorposts and counted them for fools. Imagine what happened to the Hebrews that were too afraid of looking stupid in front of their masters?"

They would have died in Egypt Demiana thought.

Demiana sat there for a moment and wondered what it meant to be in a house covered by blood. It seemed scary, knowing that the thing that saved the outsiders was the thing that showed they were outsiders. Demiana thought she should be scared, but she wasn't. For the first time since her sister put the cross around her, she was comfortable. Maybe even at peace. She reached for the thick string that carried the cross, grasped it in her palm for a moment, and pulled it out from underneath her dress shirt. Sara turned to her and smiled.

"Mom and dad are gonna be very proud," she whispered, and patted her little sister's head.

~~~

The clear glass cross was cut at an angle that reflected the sun's light in shades of purple and blue and yellow and green and red, depending on where a watcher stood. The glass lined the sides of a thin white cross laid in its core.

One of the girls in front of the door caught the flash of the cross from a few metres away and spotted Demiana and Zainab walking towards the portico. She waved them towards her.

Her name was Laila – she wore a white headscarf to school every day, although Demiana knew that was just something she did for her father. She was skinny and very pale for an Egyptian, though her eyes and brows were the darkest brown. Unlike Zainab, who had dark olive skin and light brown eyes.

"Hi girls," Laila yelled.

Zainab and Demiana waved and walked faster towards her. The three met in front of the wooden doors.

"You look lost today Zainab," Laila laughed.

"I didn't get enough sleep."

"I can tell. Your eyes are swollen. You should wash them out with honey."

"Honey's expensive. My dad would beat me with his shoe if I used it on anything other than tea or bread."

"You can use some of my honey," Demiana said.

"Thanks," Zainab said, "but I don't see how rubbing honey into my face is gonna get rid of my bags anyway."

"Well it works," Laila said. "I know. I had the same problem before."

"Come to my house tonight and we'll try it out," Demiana said. "You should come too Laila."

"I can't. I need to go home right after school. My mother made me promise I'd cook with her tonight."

"You're gonna slaughter your own chicken?" Zainab asked. Demiana and Zainab laughed.

"No!" Laila said. "My dad slaughters. I pluck. Besides, I don't see how either of you could laugh. You're both just as poor as me."

"Yeah, but I won't touch a dead chicken except to cook it," Zainab said, cringing. "I leave the cutting and plucking to my brothers."

"Shut up," Laila said. "You-"

The bell rung before she could finish. The three girls made their way in front of the door and stood in the middle of the forming line. Demiana heard the loudspeaker above her set off a shrill squeal. The national anthem played, followed by a short poem recorded off the radio by a young Alexandrian introduced as Yacoub. The girls heard the thumps and thuds of the microphone as the principal placed it in front of a cassette player and pressed play. The cassette was of Yacoub's voice reading his own poem.

> In quiet hours our Proud Nation sat
> And watched the foreigner step on our lands
> And with their nails and sharpened fangs
> Clawed into our soil and sucked the sap from our trees.

The boy's crackling, prepubescent voice reached a heightened screech at the end of each line. Demiana's mind wandered as the boy continued his rant against Western colonialism. She'd heard it too many times before.

"I think they're getting a little too serious," Zainab whispered to Laila.

The two girls tried to hold back their laugher. Demiana saw a flash of beige cut through the air and smack into the back of Zainab's bare neck. Lurching above Zainab, Ms. Safiya bent down to her level and stared into her wide eyes.

"Never, ever, ever talk during announcements," the woman said with an unflinching stare.

Zainab straightened her back and held her hand to her heart, "I'm sorry teacher. I won't do it again."

Ms. Safiya raised her head and walked to the front of the line. The recorder clacked at the end of the cassette. The microphone boomed again and the principal spoke.

"God keep Egypt in the hands of the righteous," the principal said.

A short, fat woman with a subtle hunch pushed the front doors open. Ms. Safiya took her class in first. Demiana and the rest of Ms. Safiya's grade eleven homeroom history class followed their teacher down the narrow white hallways in single file and absolute silence. Ms. Safiya opened the door and counted the girls as they walked in, one by one. Demiana made sure not to look at her as she entered, although she was tempted to wish her a good morning like her sister told her to.

Demiana took her place in the front of the class closest to the door. On the other side, the faint honey-sweet smell of sweet potato sold by street vendors lingered through the open windows. Demiana rested her legs against the steel framework of her desk, which felt cool through her dress pants. A framed picture of President Sadat hung above the front desk, as it did in every other Egyptian classroom.

Demiana hated that picture. The president's eyes always fell on her. Everywhere she sat, she could feel the heat of the Believing President's stare. Her beliefs were different from his beliefs. He knew from the cross around her neck. She was a threat to national security. Quietly, he stared and judged and held his peace.

But sometimes she wondered what Egypt would become without him. At the very least, he kept the bombs from flying over Cairo. Until that day, she had an urge to hide underneath a desk every time she heard a siren, like she was taught in 1967. Sadat hated her, but he kept her safe.

Demiana looked up at her teacher who stood above her front desk flipping through her binder. Strands of curly black hair peeked through the ends of her headscarf. She was a slender woman, although her modest pink dress shirt and black shin length skirt couldn't hide her subtle curves. She tried, but she couldn't conceal her beauty. A cold beauty as it was.

She licked her finger and turned a page in her binder, turned around towards the blackboard and wrote the day's lesson. The First Crusade. Yesterday, she'd finished off at the battle of Antioch, after the Crusaders destroyed the Turks, claimed to find a relic of the spear that pierced Jesus, and went on to the gates of Ma'arra.

"The Crusaders were diseased," she said as she wrote on the board. "And starving. They drank their own horse's blood at one point. Like animals. They stood at the gates of Ma'arra, in the name of their God, and stormed the gates and killed every Muslim man, woman and child. As we've discussed before," she turned around and examined the class, "this was not new to the Crusader barbarians. They wanted us all dead. But what happened next was far worse."

She turned her stare to Demiana, who sat with her back straight against her seat and her eyes wide. She did not want to hear what came next, but what disturbed her more was the straight, almost hostile stare the teacher set on her – an eyebrow raised slightly, lips pinched open – the face of sheltered rage.

"In the boundaries of the gates, they boiled us alive," Ms. Safiya said. "Impaled our children on spits and roasted them with the cut flesh, and ate them."

"They were cannibals?" Demiana cried. She usually didn't speak without raising her hand, she knew she'd be scolded, but she'd never heard of people eating each other before. Except in old Egyptian myths. This had to be a myth.

"Only if you define a cannibal as a human that eats humans," Ms. Safiya said. A few of the girls in her class giggled.

"That can't be!" Demiana said. "That's not human!"

Demiana realized she'd just spoken out of turn twice. Ms. Safiya, staring at her for a moment, relaxed her lips. She turned around, picked her binder up from behind her and held it up to her own face.

"Albert of Aix, a Crusader, wrote 'Not only did our troops not shrink from eating dead Turks and Saracens; they also ate dogs.'" She turned to Demiana again, with the same hostile stare. "The people who ate our flesh considered us worse than dogs."

Demiana leaned back and shrank into her seat, eyes wide and mouth open, and tried to take in her teacher's words. Centuries ago, Christian soldiers fought and killed and ate other men. And they did this under the banner of the cross. The same cross Sara told Demiana to take as the source of her hope. The same cross that hung from her neck. She remembered how heavy it was for her that first day Sara gave it to her. She could feel it digging into her shirt, its sides sharp as her teacher's tongue.

~~~

Zainab sat on Demiana's couch with her eyes closed. Demiana held a jar of honey in one hand, a piece of cardboard in the other. She dipped the cardboard into the honey and spread it over the bags underneath Zainab's eyes.

It was the sixth of October, 1981. It had been eight years to the day since Egypt crossed the Suez Canal – the government held its annual victory parade through the streets of Cairo. Demiana watched the parade on her small black and white television. This was the first time she'd watched television in her own home – her brother had bought one and set it up the night before after she fell asleep.

President Sadat rode through the streets in a black Lincoln. He stood outside through the open sunroof between two other men, vice-president Mubarak and another Demiana didn't recognize, all dressed in their green military uniforms.

"It's like watching real life," Demiana said.

"In black and white," Zainab said.

"Your eyes are closed. You can't even see anything."

"I've had television in my house for a year now. You get used to it."

"It feels like they're gonna pop out of the screen."

"You're not the only one with a parade in your house you know? Believe it or not, there are hundreds of people in the world with televisions. Thousands even."

Demiana licked the honey that dribbled off the end of the piece of cardboard after she finished spreading it on her friend's face. She set it, sticky side up, on the table next to her. She walked towards Zainab and jumped on the couch. Zainab had her eyes open now, though the honey still stuck to her face, and the two watched the procession.

Demiana's stomach had felt unsettled since homeroom history. She moved her hand up to her cross and grasped it in her palm. She wished she'd never heard of the Crusaders. She wished they never existed. She wished she could ease the weight that hung from her neck, but she knew her sister and her parents would be devastated if she did.

"Do you think I'm a Crusader?" Demiana blurted. Zainab laughed and poked at the honey underneath her eyes.

"I'm serious."

"Have you ever eaten another man's flesh?"

"I'm serious!"

"So am I. Have you ever eaten another man's flesh? I'm asking you."

"No."

"You're alright then, I think."

"You know the Crusaders had crosses on their shields."

"Symbols are what you make of them," Zainab said. "Besides, I've seen crosses on churches all over Egypt. You guys still haven't attacked." Demiana giggled.

Zainab poked at the bags under her eyes. Her fingers became wet with honey. She licked her fingers and rubbed them dry against her shirt.

"You know why Ms. Safiya's so bitter?" Zainab asked.

"Why?"

"Her husband died a few years ago. She's a thirty-something year old widow."

"Really? How'd he die?"

"Bilharzia. It was a slow death."

"Are you serious?"

"Yup. Painful too. She watched him suffer."

"How do you know?"

"My mother has a friend that lives on her street. All Ms. Safiya has left is her son."

"The fat boy that walks her to school every morning?"

"Yeah."

Demiana nodded as if she understood, but she didn't. She wondered what had changed in Ms. Safiya's life after her husband died. She wondered how her teacher got around the city – she only knew of two women on her street that drove. And how did her son get to his own school after he walked her to work? He must've walked alone, or maybe a relative picked him up from his mother's work.

Maybe she loved her husband, and maybe he loved her. Or maybe the whole marriage was a formality, its sole purpose to produce children. Maybe a lot of things. The only thing she knew for sure, Ms. Safiya still had one son. One short, fat son.

Demiana sagged into her seat and watched the parade. The tanks rolled down the streets of Suez and the camera cut to a shot of five jets in v-formation flying over the city, then down to Sadat. He sat between the same two men who stood beside him in the Lincoln, in front of a large crowd of patrons. He talked and laughed with Mubarak and smoked his pipe. Sadat watched the passing six-wheelers and cargo trucks and tanks and Humvees that rolled by in fours.

He stood up and saluted the passing convoy. Demiana noticed an object the size of a tennis ball fly towards him. She heard short spurts of what sounded like a firecracker and saw the president fall. The screen turned to static.

"What just happened?" Zainab asked, her mouth open like she was dumb.

"Was that a part of the show?"

"Oh God!"

"No," Demiana said.

"Oh God, I think they just shot him!"

"No they didn't."

"He died! They shot him!"

"No. No, it can't be. They can't show that on television."

"They shot him! Didn't you just see him fall? He's dead!"

Demiana jumped off the couch and turned off the television. She rested her palms against the table and hung her head above the antenna, more surprised than horrified. The President, the leader of Egypt, the broker of peace between the Arab world and far off enemies, might have died in their sight.

Demiana, head hung low, thought back to the day Sadat announced he released the members of the Muslim Brotherhood from prison. "He released them, then he is one of them," Sara'd told her. "He'll die by his own hands."

For a moment, a brief moment, Demiana wondered if he deserved it. Even if he did, who would protect her from the bombs now? She raised her head and turned to Zainab.

"Did they just shoot him?" Demiana asked.

"Yes!"

"Who?"

"I don't know."

Zainab went home a few minutes later, still in shock. The two girls kissed on each cheek at Demiana's door step. Zainab walked off.

Demiana spent the rest of the afternoon cooking with her mother. The radio sat between them as they cut onions on either side of the table. A man on the radio told the facts of the assassination as they came in. Between the tidbits of information on the dead president's history, he played patriotic ballads about Egypt.

"It's the President's curse," her mother said. "It happened to Nasser too. He was poisoned."

"No he wasn't." Demiana shook her head. Her mother looked up from the onions to her daughter's face. Her mother was a fat woman, her face round and dark. She wore a white scarf with a picture of St. Mina around her hair, and a slight smile on her face. Demiana knew what that smile meant. Her mother was annoyed by Demiana's challenging her.

"You don't believe me?" she asked. "They're all destined to be destroyed. The crooked ones, and they're all crooked. It's the will of God."

She tapped her palm lightly against the table. Demiana knew not to argue after that.

"So he deserved it?" Demiana asked.

"Did you see how he freed the Brotherhood? Did you see how he abolished our pope for speaking out against him? This is Egypt. This will always be Egypt. And the next one will go too, one way or the other."

"Who's gonna protect us now? The army?"

"The army?" she scoffed. "You didn't see them shoot your president right in front of you? You can't trust anyone with a name in this country."

"Then who?"

"God exists," her mother said.

Demiana wiped the tears from her eyes with a small handkerchief, she'd been cutting onions for too long. She noticed her mother's eyes hadn't even watered. She'd been cutting onions all her life.

Demiana pushed the knife away and rested her head on her palm, staring at an icon of the martyr Abu Sefein, wielding two swords above his head, behind her mother. Even great warriors could die.

She wondered if Sadat ever felt like a stranger in his own country since the peace treaty with the people that sucked the sap from their trees. A lot of people hated him after that. *Why didn't he protect himself?* she thought. He should've painted his doorpost with blood.

She walked to the kitchen to get a pot for her mother. On her way there, the telephone rang. Demiana went to the living room to pick up.

"Hello," she said.

"Demiana?" a weak voice muttered.

"Hi Zainab. How are you?"

"Demiana, I can't give you a ride tomorrow," she said.

"Oh, that's okay. Why not though?"

"I just can't," Zainab said. She sounded sad. "Not tomorrow or the next day."

"Why? What's wrong? Did I do something?"

"No, don't say that! But I won't see you tomorrow. I'm sorry."

Are you stupid a gruff voice yelled in the background. *To apologize to a Nazarene?*

"Why? What's wrong? Why is your dad yelling at you?" Demiana cried.

"I'm s-,I – I have to go." Zainab hung up. Confused, Demiana called Zainab back.

Zainab's father hung up on her when she asked to speak to his daughter.

Demiana told her mother she couldn't cook anymore that night, she had too much homework. She went to her room, dug her face into her pillow, and cried late into the night.

~~~

Word had spread quickly through the radio and television the next day. Sara was right. President Sadat had been assassinated by the Brotherhood. Egypt was under a state of emergency, and would be for the rest of the year. The whole schoolyard talked about it. One girl sat alone on the ledge and wept. A few seemed happy he was dead. But whether they loved or hated him, all feared the uncertainty of Egypt's future.

All but Demiana. She didn't care one way or the other. She walked to school alone that morning, she told her parents she was sick of riding to school every day. She stepped over bottles and old newspaper pages and used charcoal outside the shisha bars.

The streets were lined with plain grey concrete buildings. She spotted clouds floating aimlessly over the cement skyline above the buildings. The stench of cow hock pierced her senses like sharpened steel as she walked, without a car window to weaken the smell. Cairo's busy streets felt like a wasteland. The roads were dirty and the people were garbage.

Demiana arrived at the school alone. She was a few minutes early. She looked around for Zainab. She wanted to ask her what happened. She couldn't find her.

"Hi," a voice from behind her said. She turned.

"Oh, hi Laila," Demiana said and feigned a smile.

"I heard about what happened," she said. She rubbed Demiana's shoulder and faked her own smile. "I'm really sorry."

"I don't care if he's dead," Demiana said. Her cheeks flushed after she realized what she said. Luckily, only Laila heard, and she didn't care.

"I'm talking about Zainab. She came to my apartment last night. She told me what happened."

"She did?" Demiana yelled. "She told me nothing! What happened with her? Where is she?"

"I don't think she's coming back to school. Her dad found a husband for her."

"Husband? She's sixteen. She wanted to get married after university. I wanna talk to her."

"I don't think you can do that. I don't think her dad likes you. He thinks it was the Nazarenes that killed him. He said you're Mossad."

"Mossad? I don't even know what that is."

"I know."

"And doesn't he hate Sadat? One time, in the morning, we were driving and he was going on about how he wouldn't mind if someone killed him."

"He's crazy."

"Doesn't it make more sense that people who agree with him

may have killed Sadat?"

"It does, but her dad's crazy."

Demiana's head felt light. Her knees went weak. She sighed and held back her tears, and walked over to the ledge and sat. Laila followed. There was nothing she could do but sit and wish it wasn't true. Demiana watched the crowds move. f many of them didn't even stop their lives for Sadat, who would stop for a nobody like her? All she did was lose a friend.

Just last week, she'd sat on the side of the streets in a plastic beach chair with Zainab, eating peaches and contemplating how the world would end. Zainab said they'd know it was coming when the last peach tree died. "Might as well end then," she said. "That's not a world I'd wanna live in." They laughed. Those were good peaches.

She spotted Ms. Safiya a few metres away, walking towards the school. She held her little boy's hand, he couldn't have been more than ten years old. A short, fat boy with dark brown hair, a white shirt and blue suspenders. He pulled the collar of his shirt over his nose and paced in front of his mom. She tugged his arm, pulling him back. She smiled that morning. For her, in that moment, Egypt was whole. Ms. Safiya had what she needed, no matter what news played over the radio.

She walked him to a bus stop where a skinny woman in a blue dress stood. Ms. Safiya waved to the woman as she approached.

At the bus stop, she kissed the woman on each cheek and tugged the boys hand into the other woman's open palm. Ms. Safiya slouched to her son's level, kissed him on his head and stood up and waved goodbye as she walked away.

That day, Demiana understood the sting of that long goodbye. She wished Ms. Safiya didn't need to leave her boy. She looked so happy while she was with him.

The bell rang. Demiana made her way to her class line with Laila. She heard a heavy thud from the loudspeakers. After the national anthem, the principal took the microphone.

"Sadat is dead," she said, "but Egypt still stands. God keep Egypt in the hands of the righteous." That was all. For all the mourning and cursing of the killers the media showed throughout the country, that statement seemed too simple. Almost stupid. The short, fat woman opened the doors of the school and Ms. Safiya led her class in. She was straight-faced and sterile again. There was no assassination, no country in crisis in her classroom. She wouldn't allow it.

The girls took their seats behind the teacher's desk. Demiana watched Ms. Safiya look through her daily lesson plan. She wondered what Crusader atrocities she'd talk about that day. She convinced herself that nothing could be worse than Ma'arra. Impossible.

Ms. Safiya turned towards the blackboard to erase what was written the day before. The girls heard a loud honk and a dull thud and looked outside.

"Teacher!" Laila yelled. "Teacher, a boy was just hit by a car!"

Ms. Safiya dropped the blackboard eraser and rushed towards the windows along with the rest of the class.

"Oh God, don't let it be my son!" she cried.

"Don't say that teacher!" Demiana yelled. "God forbid!"

Ms. Safiya looked out the window and sighed, it was not her son, and looked back at all the girls standing behind her. Demiana knew she recognized her voice. She blushed. She didn't mean to yell what she yelled. The words came out by themselves.

Ms. Safiya stared at the shy Nazarene for a moment. Demiana noticed her raised eyebrow and open lips. Not angry this time, but confused. Ms. Safiya set off a short shudder in her body, as if trying to shake off a thought, and looked away.

"Let's go help him," she said. She sent one of the girls to the office to call the police. The rest walked outside with her towards the boy, who sat up and managed to crawl towards the sidewalk. He looked the same age as her son, but he was much darker and his hair was thick and nappy.

Ms. Safiya asked him what his name was, but he didn't answer. He didn't look like he could. The boy bled from a long gash across his left cheek that ran up his scalp. Pockets of blood soaked through his t-shirt and mixed with the mud and dust from Cairo's sandy streets. The car that hit him disappeared.

The boy couldn't hold his head in the air for very long before it fell to the ground. Ms. Safiya picked the little boy up and held him in her arms and walked back towards the school. She looked back at the class every so often, but Demiana felt like she looked back to see her. Only her. The dumbfounded stare didn't leave the teacher's face all morning.

The girls walked back to class while Ms. Safiya waited in the office for the ambulance to arrive. She came back after the paramedics picked the boy up and taught as if nothing had happened.

The content she presented that day was just as brutal as the day before, but it felt subdued to Demiana. Ms. Safiya didn't look at her every time she explained a Crusader war crime that day. Her voice had sunk and sounded more matter-of-fact. As if everything she explained belonged to another time.

The hour passed quickly and she ended her class. "Tomorrow, how we took back Jerusalem. Go."

Demiana stood up and packed her bag. She was the slowest bag-packer in her class, almost always the last to leave. After everyone had gone, she threw her bag over her shoulder and walked towards the door.

"Demiana," Ms. Safiya called. She turned towards the teacher. "Come here."

She took a few slow steps towards the front desk where Ms. Safiya sat. Demiana stopped a foot away from her after she spotted the wooden ruler that hung off the side of the front desk. *She can't hit me* she thought. *Not in high school.*

"Yes teacher?"

"You yelled in class today."

"Yes teacher. I'm sorry."

"Why?"

"I didn't mean to."

"I didn't ask if you meant to or not. I asked why."

Demiana stared at the wooden ruler in front of her and breathed in. Breathed out. She considered what answer would let her go the quickest. In her panic, all she could think of was the truth.

"I said why!"

"That could've been your son!" she cried with the same urgency as the outburst that got her in trouble.

Ms. Safiya stared at her for a moment. Demiana's body felt heavy, weighed down by her teacher's eyes.

"Thank you," Ms. Safiya said.

"What?"

"For what you said. That's my only son."

Demiana stood in a daze. She shook her head to say you're welcome.

"I'll see you tomorrow?"

"Yes teacher."

Demiana turned towards the door and made her way outside. She sat on the alabaster ledge, as she did everyday between classes, and kicked her feet against its side. Zainab was gone, and Egypt didn't care. But at least Ms. Safiya's son wasn't hit by a car.

Maybe Zainab will have a son someday Demiana thought. Maybe she'd meet Zainab again in the future, and Zainab would have a house and a stove and maybe even a car. And her own son she'd walk to school every day. And Demiana would meet her at a bus stop and they'd kiss on each cheek and she'd take the little palm of Zainab's little boy.

Demiana stared up at the wide, clear skies and watched a plane fly up higher and higher still until it disappeared above the clouds. *Keep going* she thought as the plane approached the sun. *You're almost there.*

MOSES THE BLACK

I saw the colour of heat on Cairo's city streets the day the doctor told me I was going blind. The jagged lines that rode between bricks across buildings and the shades of everything bright hot and alive struck me for the first time.

I stared through the thin patches of grass that grew between the broken pieces of cement and brown stalks of palm trees rising from and covering the ground with their massive fronds like owners of the land and the colour of the people that hovered below in all different shapes. Everyone walked like they had somewhere to be. I wondered if they ever recognized each other.

Mama held my hand and walked me through the streets. "Everything'll be alright" she smiled and tried to mean it. She told me to unbutton my collar because I was sweating. I was too busy watching time move to listen. She stopped, knelt down and pulled me toward her as she reached for my collar. I saw myself in the brown of her eye. My head looked round and glossy, like a balloon on a string held down by a brick.

"Soon you'll have beautiful blue eyes," she spoke quietly like a secret. There were words stuck in her throat. If she said what she needed to, we could move. I needed to move. Her eyes were too wide and heavy for me to stare too long.

I looked down at her neck. Her crystal cross beamed purple from where I stood. I tilted my head slightly and watched it turn blue to red to orange to green.

"Maybe the doctor was wrong," I said for her sake, smiling like a good boy. She pursed her lips and smiled with a hope and a lie. She patted my shoulders and stood up, took my hand, and we walked away. I watched the colours fly through the streets.

At the street corner sat an old man in a moustache and galabeya, his face worn and etched. Dark brown skin like a Southerner. He sat cross-legged on a thin white blanket in front of a basket made of palm leaves full of fish and stabbed at one with scales that shined like steel in the sun. He carved out something pink from its gut and threw it in a plastic bag in front of him, wrapped the fish in a sheet of old newspaper and handed it to a woman that stood to his side.

Mama dragged me to the fish man at the street corner by my sleeve. He aged with each step. Lines dug deep into his skin under his tired eyes. Light patches of stubble grew around his moustache and into his sunken cheeks. His graven face, weak and powerless and angry and alive.

The man watched us approach with his eyes on me. I looked into his basket when we got there. It was full of black fish with long whiskers. Beside him was a tin bucket with the same kind of fish, but these ones were alive and swimming.

"How much for the catfish," mama asked.

"Which one?"

Mama pointed one out in the basket.

"Why do you want a basket fish? I got live fish right here woman," he pointed at the bucket. "I don't always bring live fish with me you know? They haven't even felt air yet."

"Those are more expensive."

"Why do you care about price? You got a growing boy here." He nodded at me. "Don't you wanna see him grow big and healthy? God bless you little boy."

Mama stared at me for a moment, then back at the man. She pointed to a large fish in the bucket. It swam away from her finger.

The man gave her a price. She bargained him down by a few pounds. He leaned over into the bucket and grabbed the fish out with his hands. It flung its tail and shook its head from side to side open mouthed as it drowned in the open air.

"Head on or off?" the man asked.

"Off," mama said.

The man slammed the anxious fish onto a slab of wood, picked up a large knife to his side and cut its head off clean. The bent tail slowly fell and rested on the wood. He put the head on an old piece of newspaper and handed it to me.

"There you go guy," the man said as I took it from his hands.

I stared at it for a moment. It stared back with tiny hollow black eyes, its mouth wide. It didn't look much different from when it was alive. I examined it from the inside, saw where its pink flesh married bone under its skin.

He gutted the fish body while mama and I hovered above him.

"You're good," I told the man. He nodded and smiled at the ground.

"This is my life."

"You cut it real nice."

"I've been doing this for twenty years guy. Catch, cut, sell."

The man put the knife down, pulled a cigarette from out of his pocket, lit it and pushed it between his lips.

"You have no idea what these things can do," the man said wriggling his fingers.

I shook my head and stared at his rough hands. A large gash stitched and pink dug from his wrist and twisted up beneath his tattered sleeve. The man finished gutting the fish, rolled it in some newspaper and handed it to mama.

"Maybe I could work for you?" I said. The man laughed and so did mama.

She said thank you and pushed my head away from the man and told me we needed to go.

"I don't give money," the man yelled. I looked back. "But I take volunteers." He winked. Mama walked faster.

We lived right around the block. It took a few minutes to walk home. Baba was sitting on the couch reading a newspaper waiting for us. He put down the paper and asked mama what the doctor said.

Glaucoma. What a stupid word.

I made my way to my room while they talked and stared at myself in the mirror.

The world had changed just about a month ago. Every so often, I saw halos around streetlights. I woke up with a dull throbbing in my eyes almost every morning. The headaches burned small holes in my sight where all I could see were traces of white hidden between patches of the world.

But my eyes looked the same as I remembered them. White on the outside, round and dark and brown in the middle. They shined under the light. I wondered how things could change but still look the same.

I sat up on my bed and stared at the icon of St. Moses the Black mama bought from a monastery while she was pregnant with me. Another killer reborn and saved. Dark skin. Dark eyes. A halo around his white knotted hair offering his rusted heart in his palm to the sun. And his hands, those ragged hands stained by old blood, some from his worn sodden heart.

I heard mama in the other room whispering to baba. She didn't want me to hear and I didn't want to hear her. I closed the door of my room and sat on my bed staring at my palms, clenching and unclenching my fists, small but heavy, and I knew they were real.

~~~

I saw the fish man on the street corner on my way home from school the next day. I walked up to him before he could spot me.

"You said you'd take volunteers."

The man looked up at me and ran his grime stained fingernails over his thick stubble, a cigarette in his right hand, and winced.

"You can't take a joke?" he said and rested both arms on his legs.

"I didn't know that was a joke."

"You probably don't know a lot of things."

"I know you don't own the street corner." The man looked up and took a drag.

He looked back at the passing cars. I took a seat a few feet away from him. The many men and women and cars and stray dogs and cats and children and rats felt heavy from where I sat, like I carried the congestion of the streets on my shoulders with all its stench. It was hard to notice another person's scent in Cairo because the smell of the city's streets lingered in every corner, but I could smell the man. He smelled like a wet dog.

He turned to me.

"What's your name boy?"

"Moses. What's yours?"

"Moses?" the man asked. "The man who split the sea."

"No not that Moses. Mama named me after Moses the Black."

"Moses the Black?"

"Yeah. He was a bad man."

The fish man cocked his head back against the wall and laughed.

"Mama named you after a bad man?"

"Well, he died a good man. Mama loved him because he did some good things. But he did a lot of bad things before he changed."

"That's okay. I was a bad man too."

"How were you bad?" I asked.

He rested one palm on his knee caps and rubbed the other on his thigh. The man nodded and rolled his eyes to a corner and stared for a moment. He cocked the bottom half of his jaw forward and bit his lower lip. I wondered what he was thinking.

"My name is Marwan," he said.

"Mr. Marwan," I said. "How were you bad?"

The man smirked to himself and wiped the sweat off his carved brow.

"You don't see my trail of dead?" he said as he directed my sight to his fish with an open palm to the sky. All of his fish laid lifeless in a basket.

"Why didn't you get your bucket of fish? The alive ones."

The man wiped his damp hands on his galabeya.

"You know, yesterday was the only day I ever tried that," he said shifting his eyes between me and the streets. "I thought it would make me money for being the only guy in Cairo stupid enough to sell live fish. The cab driver made me pay him for the water I spilled on his seats. I lost money that day."

"Well I thought it was a good idea."

"That's why I call you guy."

"I wanna work for you."

He laughed and sat back.

"Shouldn't you be home soon?"

"Mama and baba don't finish work for another few hours."

"I don't have money for you, you know?"

"I don't want your money," I said. "I want your hands."

The man stared at me and smiled, measuring my words to my size.

"You grow old, learn to work, cut and be cut. Your hands will be like my hands."

Mr. Marwan smelled like an old dog in the rain. That's what baba called street vendors. Dogs.

It was strange seeing the streets from where he sat. The people hovered above me like clouds. I sat so low I saw the dirt under their shoes. They all looked so different, but they felt the same.

"It's like the ocean," I said.

The man turned and looked at me.

"What is?"

"The people. They all move the same way."

The man breathed in and shook his head as the people passed.

"Not the ocean," he said.

"I think they are."

"No. They're ghosts. This city is haunted." He looked at me and smiled.

"Ghosts?"

"Yeah. You see how they float? You see how they pass each other like nobody else exists? None of them exist. That's why they can't see nothing but themselves."

He rested his shoulders. "Maybe they can't even see themselves."

"What about you?"

"What about me?"

"Do you exist?"

The man leaned forward and stared at me.

"Look at me. Look at my eyes. Do I look alive to you?"

The lines below his narrow dark brown eyes burrowed deep within his gaunt flesh. They cut through deeper creases that carved his barren cheeks. His neck covered in sun spots and rough skin extended from his tired shoulders like an old tree stump that stood on principle, a forced strength.

"Yes," I said. "You have to be alive to see a ghost."

"And you see them too," Mr. Marwan said as he touched the ends of his thumbs together and crossed his fingers. He leaned forward and smiled a half-smile as if he knew something no one else did. He grabbed a fish and started to cut.

"I've watched these people float for years you know? How they move. How they bump into each other and curse and move on. You know how many times I've seen men cop a feel of a woman they don't know, and play it off like nothing happened? In broad daylight too. Almost always at bus stops when they think nobody's watching. A lot of times the woman pretends nothing happened. Can you believe that? A dirty man gropes you from behind and you shrug it off."

"People are disgusting."

"I don't think they think anybody cares enough to notice. But I do," he said as he scraped out intestines. "I sit. I watch. I wait. Like a lion."

"A lion."

"Yes. There's a time for everything. A time to hurt and a time to heal. A time to break and a time to build. God's words. And I've already been broken," he said. "I'm just waiting for my time to move in on the kill," he said and laughed. I think he had to laugh to convince me he was joking.

I shrugged and sat silent and watched the crowd. A spirit slept beneath the man's words. A horrible truth I didn't know. I looked down to my palms and twiddled my thumbs and clasped the fingers of both my hands together and looked back up, resting my chin against my knuckles.

"I think a lion lives inside my head."

"You and me both," he said.

A man with a trim beard and fine blue suit approached us. His hair nappy and short, black with a patch of white on his right temple. He was a tall man, maybe six foot and bulky like a gorilla.

"Fish man," he said with weighted words, as if his talk alone was strong. "What do you have?"

"It's your lucky day," Mr. Marwan said. "I've just cut and gutted a few, still fresh."

The man examined the prepared fish to Mr. Marwan's side.

"No," he said. "I want from the ones you've still never touched. I want three."

"What's wrong with these?"

The bearded man stared at Mr. Marwan for a moment, his eyes narrow and sharp. His mouth curved down slightly, as if he was upset with the fish man dragging him into a conversation. He had places to be.

"How do I know where your hands have been?"

"The hands that cut the fish you don't want are the same hands that caught the ones you do sir," Mr. Marwan said.

"Yeah but these ungutted ones have less fingerprints right? I know you're a busy man fishing and catching and gutting every day, it's probably hard to find time to wash I assume. No?"

"Are you calling me dirty, sir?"

"No. I'm not God to judge. I just know you're a busy man. Washing costs time and time costs money. I'm a business man too. I know these things. I can't blame you for not spending time you don't have on cleaning yourself. I'll gut my own fish and save you time. These gutted fish will go to the next man."

Mr. Marwan thought for a moment. He gave the bearded man a price.

"That's a high price for three catfish."

"Yes, but I don't bargain on my fish. Time costs you know?" Mr. Marwan smiled. "We're both businessmen here."

The man reached for his wallet reluctantly. "You're lucky I've got places to be," he said, and paid the asking price. Mr. Marwan folded each catfish in old newspaper and put them in a plastic bag.

"Salam," he said. The bearded man didn't respond. He stared at me funny, like I wasn't supposed to be there.

"Is that your son?" he asked.

"This is my future," Mr. Marwan said. The man nodded and walked away.

"You think I'm your future?"

"No. But it's none of his business who you are."

I watched Mr. Marwan sell out all the fish in his basket within the next hour.

"I'm done," he said.

I nodded.

"I'm not giving you any money."

"I don't want money."

He stood up and wiped the dirt off his galabeya and picked up his basket and walked away. I said goodbye but he wouldn't turn around or wave. I waited until he disappeared into the crowds before I stood up and made my way home.

~~~

I walked into my room and closed the door behind me. St. Moses hovered above my mirror and stared down at me.

"Did you ever feel like you missed the darkness?" I asked him. "After you gave it up?" He stared at me, angry at my question and offering his heart.

~~~

Mama administered my eye drops before I slept that night. She hugged me and kissed me and tucked me in and then I was gone.

I woke up after a time, maybe a half hour, with a bad headache that came every so often since my eyes started to play tricks. I laid in the dark and blocked my ears with my hands from the street noise. That didn't work.

Flying shapes and colours flashed in front of me with every thud against my skull. I held the part of my head where I felt the pounding and rolled side to side on my bed, praying for mercy. I tried to wipe the flying things away from me hoping my headache would go away once they did, but they soaked through my hand. I closed my eyes so they'd stop existing. They didn't.

I threw up that night. My gagging woke mama. She ran to the bathroom. When she got there, her eyes wide and bloodshot, she patted me on my back as I hurled with my head above the toilet. I tod her about the flying shapes. She said she was so sorry for what had happened. I told her she didn't need to be. Mama wiped my chin with toilet paper. I felt a lot better after I threw up. My headache left. She kissed me goodnight and walked me to my bed and tucked me in to sleep again.

~~~

I saw Mr. Marwan the next day. I walked over to where he sat. I sat in the same spot as the day before and turned to the crowd.

"You're back," he said, staring at the intestines of a fish he was cutting.

"If you're here, I'm coming."

I watched him cut the belly of the fish. He was smooth and true in the lines he carved, his whole motion in his wrist. The fish man worked on a beat like there was a soundtrack in his mind playing to his massacre.

"What if you couldn't see?"

The man turned to me.

"You mean like if I was blind?"

"Yeah."

"Why?"

I wanted to tell him about my eyes but I feared the words themselves – how they'd feel as they came out. I could see them in my mind with their shape and colour.

I-

am going-

Blind.

The words were too exact, too sharp to spill without cutting me.

"Just asking."

The man finished the fish and set it to a side by itself in his large basket. He rested his back on the wall and sighed and looked to the sky. Maybe he'd thought of this already. He didn't think he'd need to remember.

"If I were blind, I would still go down to the river every morning. I'd feel my way onto the boat. I'd paddle to the centre of the water. I'd know I was in the centre because that's when my arms start to get tired. I'd hook a worm to the hook and draw my line with my eyes open to the blackness all around me. I'd wait for the fish to bite and then reel it in. You don't need eyes to feel. I'd throw it in a basket beside me. I'd do that again and again until the fish stopped biting. Then I'd row back to shore. I'd take a taxi out to the big city. You don't need to see taxi drivers. You can smell them. I'd set up shop on the floor where I could feel the heat of the people. I'd hack out the fish's insides in front of the crowds, just because I could. And I'd spit on the face of any man who asked to help me."

"How would your hands know where to go when you're cutting a fish?"

"If you do it for long enough, it's like breathing." He picked up a fish and closed his eyes.

"You feel the scales," he said, running his fingers over the fish's underbelly. "Cut from the lowest part of its body." He ran the knife smoothly through the fish's skin. "And on down until the head. You know the head by the feel of the gills and the eyes and sometimes the whiskers. You feel ahead with your thumb."

The man poked inside the fish with a knife and he cut and he scraped and he pulled its insides out. He opened his eyes and looked at the guts in his cupped hand.

"All the bad stuff," he said with a glow of pride at the bloody pearl in his palm. "I don't need eyes to know I did it right."

"Can I try?"

"Not unless you're gonna buy the fish you cut."

"But I-,"

"No."

Mr. Marwan sat there, and for the first time since I'd seen him, he looked satisfied. I wasn't sure with what. He was the only man I knew who understood something from the inside, with all its blood and guts and everything evil. He didn't find it disgusting. He worked to cut it out.

"That's the world. Skill and blood." The man turned to me and smiled a child's smile. "You cut when you need to cut."

"Fish man!" a heavy voice carved through our conversation. I looked up, and there stood the bearded man from the day before, today in a grey suit. He held a bag with a cooked catfish in his hand, a piece of flesh from its stomach cut out and exposed to the sun. As he approached, I saw the colony of tiny worms in its belly, alive and festering.

"You sell me fish with parasites, you dog."

"Sir, I didn't-"

"Stand up and talk to me," he growled. "You animal. Get up. Be more than just a dirty street vendor and get up and look me in my eye when I talk to you. Like a man."

I felt my heart beat jolt, harder and faster with the man's approaching steps. I saw Mr. Marwan secure a small knife in a hidden side pocket of his galabeya. His face as still and dark and sombre as the moment I'd met him. No fear.

"Sir, I did not mean to sell you a fish with parasites," he said with his usual cool.

"Get up I said."

"Why do I need to get up sir?"

The man threw the bag in the face of Mr. Marwan. He bent down, grabbed Mr. Marwan from underneath each armpit and picked him up to his feet and slammed him against the wall behind him. The bearded man stood several inches taller than Mr. Marwan. On his way up, the little knife Mr. Marwan packed in his pocket fell to the ground. The bearded man looked too angry to notice. I snuck the knife behind his feet and into my own pocket and stood up with them.

"Why are you doing this?" I said quietly, my mouth open and dumb. People passing the scene looked in and walked slower.

"You know what the problem with you people is?" the man asked, clasping the fabric of Mr. Marwan's galabeya in a knot over his chest, a finger pointed to his face with his other hand. "You don't know you're dirty. You don't understand how little you mean to society. How much you don't matter. They could get any garbage man to do your job. You can be replaced by a child. This child matter of fact," he motioned his head towards me, "at any time. And then where would you be? On the streets begging? Like a dog. It's not that far from where you are right now is it?"

"Sir," Mr. Marwan started, his face slowly changing. His eyebrows lowered and eyes narrowed. "You chose those fish. If I had gutted them, I could have checked for parasites myself, and threw a bad fish away. But you chose to take the risk."

"So, this is my fault then?"

"You said that."

A small crowd grew in a half-circle around us, cut off by the wall behind Mr. Marwan's back. The bearded man slowly unclenched and let loose the fabric in his fist and turned to the people.

"What do you people think?" he yelled and presented his palm to the crowds.

"What's the problem?" a short lean man said approaching the big man from amongst the growing crowd.

"I bought three fish from him yesterday. I was in a rush to go home because I was tired and had to wake up early for work, so I paid the high price he asked. I didn't bargain. And I brought the fish home to my wife, she baked it, and we ate. My wife cut a piece of fish off before she took a bite, and look what I found," he picked up the bag with the now rotten fish and waved it in the face of the people. "Parasites."

Some in the audience laughed. Others gagged at the scene of the decaying worm-ridden fish.

"So what should I do with this man? This dog."

"You chose that fish," Mr. Marwan said.

"I know that's disgusting," the short man said as he walked slow towards the scene. "I don't think he meant it." He stepped between the big man and Mr. Marwan. "The man's just barely above a beggar. Have mercy on him. It's not his fault he's ignorant."

"I'll teach him for his ignorance," the bearded man said and pushed the short man from between them, dropped the bag, and with his wide, thick open palm held to the sun, he slapped Mr.

Marwan. Mr. Marwan fell to the ground with the motion of the man's open palm and grabbed his cheek. He let go and a dark pink kissed his skin. His eyes were wide and bloodshot and a tear had rolled down his cheek. His stare searched the streets, I imagined for help or compassion or justice.

"Stop," I yelled, my eyes glazed. I wanted to grab the bearded man's hand or push him away. I stood paralyzed in my fear.

"Shut your son up," the man yelled.

The short man tried again to work his way between the two.

"Basha, I can see you love God and you're angry. Allah calls for mercy ya basha. He's just an ignorant fish man. Your gonna kill a stupid man who barely knows his right from his left. Is this what God wants?"

"Eye for an eye," the big man said as he shoved the short man out of the way.

"Sir," Mr. Marwan said. "Sir I'm sorry, but please stop."

"He's crying," a man yelled from the crowds. "Beat him!"

Some of the crowd cheered. Others gasped and yelled at him to stop. The big man in the middle approached Mr. Marwan while he was on the ground and kicked him in his gut.

"You feed my family parasites you dog? So I will treat you like a dog."

Mr. Marwan grabbed his stomach and tried to contain his tears that flowed freely and darkened the broken grey asphalt beneath him to black. The big man opened the plastic bag and held the fish in his hands.

"I should have known the dog would give me worms," he said as he shoved the fish in Mr. Marwan's face. He tried to force Mr. Marwan's mouth open as he rubbed the fish's flesh in his face. Mr. Marwan spat out the little that entered his lips. The bearded man threw the fish to the side again.

"Get up," he yelled. "Show these people your bravery." He picked Mr. Marwan up again. Mr. Marwan's eyes focused on the cool grey ground. The people worked their way closer to the two men. The crowd swallowed me in. I'd become one of them.

"Look me in my eyes you dog," the man commanded. "Before I hurt you, look up at me."

Mr. Marwan contained his pain as best as he could, still looking to the ground, and watched his tears fall.

"Look at me!"

Mr. Marwan freed his hands from his gut. He wiped the tears from his eyes, then wiped them on his galabeya. He took a deep breath.

"Beat him!" one yelled.

"Have mercy!" another.

"Throw the beggar to the wall!"

The crowd stood close. I was in the front to the big man's side, now completely unnoticeable.

The man, with two fingers in his right hand, placed them under Mr. Marwan's chin and slowly lifted it towards his eyes. Mr. Marwan tilted his head up to look at him.

His bloodshot eyes worn and forced open. He breathed a heavy breath and licked his lower lip. The rhythm of his breath slowed and hushed.

"You have," Mr. Marwan started between infrequent pants, "no honour."

The man took off his black leather shoe. He pushed Mr. Marwan from the neck against the wall a second time with his left arm, and raised the shoe above his head with his right. With the face of a rabid dog, he barked.

"Honour," the word came out jagged. "I'll show you honour."

His shoe came down fast and strong. Mr. Marwan fell to the floor as the heavy hand of Egyptian justice struck him over and over. Some in the crowd were ecstatic. They waited for blood. The man struck Mr. Marwan on the nose and it bled. His cheek ripped open and the skin around his right eye reddened and swelled.

A part of the crowd, I'd become a ghost. Nobody noticed me or cared to. They didn't see when I reached for the small knife in my pocket. I ran my thumb along its sharp end and felt it cut me. I sensed the warmth of my own blood against my skin.

I pulled it out of my pocket and held it to my side.

"Stop me God," I prayed.

Between the heat of the people and the gorilla that stood to my side, I swiftly ran the tiny blade into the fat of his flank. He roared and reached for the growing black stain on his side. He fell to his knees and stared open mouthed at his torn, bloody suit jacket. I slipped between the crowds, realizing no one had much idea what had happened.

The evening heat and the smell of the people and their sweat and the blood on my hand, the knife I snuck back into my pocket, still wet, still thirsty, and the streets and the sound of chaos and car horns and jeering and cheering and anger and the stench of violence and the taste of justice crushed me in that moment. Police sirens wailed behind me as I ran home. My stomach heaved and a headache came on slow but true.

Logic fought my heart that tried to convince me this could all be an illusion. A horribly vivid dream. Was that not the sharp end of justice poking at me from my jean pocket as I ran? Was that not my own blood dripping from my thumb, mixing with the blood on my knuckles from the gorilla?

This was real. I heard and I saw and I smelled and felt it.

"Why did you let me?" I prayed.

I made it home before my parents got back. From my balcony, I watched the ambulance drive off from the street corner and into the sunset as the crowds dispersed. A few police men stayed to interview onlookers and examine the scene. A wide black puddle slowly dried on the grey cement. I walked back to my room terrified of the old saint's quiet eyes.

I sat on my bed with my body towards the icon and my head towards the ground.

"I'm sorry. I want to look at you but I can't," I said. "I didn't know what to do. I didn't want to see my friend suffer like that. I had to save him. He did nothing."

St. Moses saved himself in his quiet.

"I just, I don't know what's real anymore."

I felt the man stare at me with his tired eyes offering his old black heart. I'd always thought he wanted to give it to me. He didn't. He wanted me to see what he once was. I wished he'd look somewhere else. I didn't need to see.

I wouldn't look up. He offered but I kept my head in my hands and wished he'd turn around. The world around me was tired. I didn't want it. I didn't know what was true and what wasn't. It didn't matter anymore. But his eyes still searched me. The black man of the desert. Lie to me. Tell me it never happened.

I opened my eyes. Traced my stare across the lifelines on my palms to the dirty floor to the wall and up to the ceiling and I watched the fan spin and lowered my stare back down to the saint's face, once at peace.

I saw his anger and felt my ribs fold in. I saw his understanding like he'd known me. As if he lived my life. I saw his hurt having known what I'd done and I saw his sin for the first time because it was my own.

My mind grew heavy and tired from everything that happened and everything I lived through. I could justify my actions, but my stomach felt like it was gradually eating itself. I rested my head on my mattress and fell asleep.

My body rested but my mind refused. The whole scene replayed in my dreams. All I could focus on was my friend on the concrete with his own blood in his palm and the bearded man's blood in mine.

∾∾∾

I woke up in a cold sweat. My body was so hot I needed to go back out to the balcony to breathe.

My alarm clock flashed 3:30. I heard baba snore. I walked out onto the balcony and stared and hung my head above the railing. I looked up above the concrete skyline and saw the white lights lining the streets stretch to infinity. I heard the whistle of a bird and another sing back its own song. I tried to control my tired mind stuck in the moment I would never get back. I stood with my head held above the railing and looked into the blackness dotted by white lights.

I hoped the big man didn't die. More importantly, I hoped my friend Mr. Marwan was still alive. I didn't think a gash on his cheek could kill him.

I sat on a beach chair on my balcony and kept my eyes open to the horizon. No sign of day still, but I knew it would come. My beating heart rushed with my thoughts and the coming colour of the streets. I saw the darkness and the cuts of streetlights across the narrow roads and I saw the gleam of cars as they passed in the synthetic light and the moon that sat perched like an ornament in an empty sky and I saw the void in this city blind to itself and I saw the world for what it was for so many more nights until I could see no more.

BREATHE LIFE

Relics of the saints rested in small red velour pouches across the front of the church. Martino sat in his mother's arms as she reached to touch the glass and muttered a blessing under her breath. She rubbed the glass, kissed her fingers and crossed herself. Martino tried to stretch for the glass like his mom but his stubby arms couldn't reach. He settled for petting the small gold cross on a thin silver chain around his mother's wrist, reached his fingers to his mouth and kissed them.

An old icon of a wide eyed, round headed bronze, skinned St. George sat proud on a white horse with a thin lance in both his hands that pierced through the mouth and into the throat of the dragon at his feet, its blood seeping from the back of its head. An angel hovered over the head of the saint readying a crown above him. His mother told him it was the crown of martyrdom.

Crown of martyrdom? The boy was too young to understand and too tired to care. Just hours ago he was home in the comfort of his room playing police chase with his toy cars. The cops always caught the bad guys before he went for a cookie break. He marched into the living room with a small red Camaro in his hand and saw his mom balancing a lamp shade on her head. She stood still in the light of the bulb beside her. The boy could tell she fought a wide smile. Tino laughed and grabbed at her leg.

"You caught me," she said. He always did. She picked up the chunky boy in her skinny arms and kissed him and walked him to the kitchen. He rested his head against her pink cotton shirt she always wore at home. He loved to rub his tubby nose against the fabric and feel her warmth. She fetched him a cookie and sat him on the table next to her chair. He faced her as he chewed and looked into the depths of her blue eyes against her bronze skin, like an oasis between the sands of the Sahara. She was the only Egyptian he'd seen with blue eyes in his few short years, aside from his own of course.

"So now that I got you here, I should tell you," his mom started. "We're moving."

"Moving where?" the boy asked. "Cairo with Uncle George?"

"No, Tino," she said as she rubbed the side of the boy's belly. "It's much further than that."

"How much further?"

"Canada. You're going to sit next to me on the plane."

"Canada? What's that?"

"You know America? Barack Obama and Fast and the Furious and all those other movies you like?"

"We're going to America?"

"Almost. Canada is right above America. It's like America's hat. Baba was accepted and we're moving in February. Isn't that exciting?"

"No! What about school?"

"There's schools in Canada."

"What about my friends?"

"Habibi, there's a lot of people in Canada you can make friends with. We're moving close to Aunt Salwa and Uncle John. Remember they visited last year with your cousins Peter and Heidi?"

"I didn't love Heidi."

"I didn't expect you to, but at least you and Peter were friends. He's your age and we'll be in the same city. You can see him whenever you want," she smiled and tickled the fat underneath his round chin.

"But what if no one else there likes me? I don't speak English."

"You'll learn."

"And what if a big white snow bear sees us when I'm walking. I could get eaten like in that movie," the boy said as he clutched at his mother's wrist. She chuckled and slid him off of her.

"Habibi," she said. "I already told you your angel is watching. You will always be protected. Even if a snow bear tries to eat you."

"You always talk about an angel but I never see it."

"Then you haven't been looking. You'll see your angel one day habibi. And you'll know."

"How?"

"When you know, you know," she said.

The boy smiled. His mother had a way with him.

Tino slid off the table onto his mother's lap and jumped to the ground. He ran back to his room to play with his toys until his father told him to dress for church.

~~~

He'd slept through much of New Year on his mother's lap during the liturgy. He woke a few times to smell the sweet char of incense and hear the deacons sing words he barely understood in a melody so full of peaks and troughs he could never grasp against a polyrhythmic backdrop of triangle and cymbals that held the chant together so loosely the boy sometimes felt the words would collapse.

The words never collapsed. The moments when he was awake, he could hear the words float from above his head to the top of the dome of the church where they echoed back down. The boy never fully understood the chanting, but it calmed him, always managed to put him right to sleep.

He woke again to a slowing chant nearing the end of the service. The boy wiped his face from the water, rubbed his eyes and yawned. On almost any other night he would've been fast asleep in his bed four hours earlier, no interruptions aside from the occasional bathroom break. At eight years old, he'd grown and learned not to pee in his sleep. The fear of his father's shoe forced his change.

"Are we done yet?" Martino muttered in his mother's ear, a narrow peak of his pupil peered through his rested eyelids. "I'm really tired."

"Yes habibi," she said. "It's past twelve. Happy New Year," she smiled and ran her fingers through his coarse hair. "Let me just go quickly to the bathroom. When I come back you can go find baba and tell him to meet me at the front okay?"

The boy nodded and laid down, his head against the seat of the wooden pew. He couldn't wait to be back home in his blue striped pajamas between the warmth of his blanket and bed.

"Holy Holy Holy," the priest and deacons and congregation sang coming to the end of the anaphora. "Heaven and earth are full of your glory." Martino heard the clang of the cymbals gradually slow to the end of a chant that he wished would go on just a little longer. At least until his mother came back. He felt his eyes gently close again.

A deep rumble with the rage of thunder startled his tired eyes wide open. The red velour drapes that separated the altar from the rest of the church had blown forward like the sail of a ship caught in a sudden storm. The boy's pew quaked underneath him. He saw the floating crystal chandelier above the altar swing and whirl from side to side from the impact of the sound that came from outside. He could barely hear it screech over the screams of the people scrambling through their pew and out towards the exit.

"Don't fear!" the priest cried in his deep raspy voice. "Don't fear! There's nothing." He waved the sign of the cross on the crowd with his right hand as they ran towards the exit. The boy caught the confusion and thought of his mom. The tips of his fingers had grown cold in the moment. He needed her to hold him and keep him warm and safe from the sound he didn't know.

A FACE LIKE THE MOON

Martino slid off the pew to his feet and towards the aisle being rushed by the rabble. His breathing became quick and shallow as he pushed through the feet of the ladies that stood between him and his mother. He needed to make it to the bathroom.

In the midst of panic, fear changed the boy's physical world. The late night winter warmth dissipated and transformed into something thick and hot. An older lady with wide dark brown eyes grabbed the boy and asked him if he was okay, her hair covered by a scarf with a large stitch of St. Mark. "I'm looking for mama," he shrieked as he wriggled her hand off his shoulder. He licked at his upper lip and tasted salt from his sweat or the tears that rolled down his cheek, or both. He couldn't tell. He wiped his wet face and pushed on.

The further he pushed through the crowd towards the bathrooms, the closer he got to the exit, the louder and more piercing the shrieks of the people became.

"Yassou!" he heard repeatedly from more than one voice. "Have mercy!"

Martino wanted to be next to his mother, but he knew she would never let him out of the front doors to see what had happened when she spotted him. If anything, she'd blind him with her palm as he sat in her arms so that he wouldn't have to see whatever was out there, like she often did whenever they passed roadkill on the highway. If he wanted to explore, he needed to do so before she spotted him.

The boy passed the ladies bathroom, making sure to hide behind the legs of the crowds that grew in the front foyer, his eyes wide from the frenzy around him. He squirmed through the people and found the two front doors, maybe twelve feet tall engraved with Coptic crosses stacked from the bottom to the top. They stood open to the streets.

Martino stepped and slipped on what felt like a wet floor. He fell against a lady's leg right onto his bottom. The boy stretched his arm across the floor to give him a base to stand on. He stood and checked his wet hands, his fingertips to his palm painted crimson. He looked down at the floor and saw patches of shoeprints in the same deep red running in and out of the church. The prints darkened and dried as he approached the outside. He wiped his hands on his white dress shirt and walked where he knew he shouldn't, until he reached the doors and peered out.

Battling alarms set off on many cars echoed through a night air so dense the boy could feel it fill his lungs. A severed hand laid palm up with its finger pointing towards the streets, welcoming him. He gasped and stepped away towards the road to distance himself from the hand. A man's torso laid a few feet from where he stood, the corpse's back full of bloody holes punctured through his shirt faced the boy, its head slightly severed from its body lying in a pool of its own blood. One of the man's legs lay a few feet from the body. The boy couldn't spot the other.

Bodies and parts of bodies graced the church entrance, at peace in their stillness. The boy too scared to cry and too dumb to turn back walked on through the corpses. He felt his lunch work its way up his insides. He felt afloat in the massacre, as if he swam through the ocean of bodies with his head barely above the bloody sea.

He stopped at the feet of a lady knelt beside a young boy, his eyes wide and dumb to the light above him. His hair was coarse and black. His lips parted as if he had something to say but couldn't. The boy looked much like Martino. The lady on her knees prayed this was just a horrible dream. She prayed for the boy to wake.

"Let him live Jesus," she cried as she tried to shake the boy awake. His body shook powerless against her force. She buried her head in his chest and wept for a moment as she muttered something to the Virgin.

The lady held her son's head with one hand and pressed down on his heart with two fingers in the other. Blood drained from his head to her fingers to her forearm and dripped in a small puddle underneath her elbow on the cool concrete. She picked him up and ran inside the church.

Martino raised his head to the streets and spotted a small car glinted green in the streetlight flipped upside down, lying on its hood as smoke floated from its trunk and dissipated into the black night. All around him people crept between bodies and cried and some cursed under their breath as they wept. All but one woman, who stood under a large wooden painting of a bronze Jesus who held his arms open to the streets, spattered with the blood of the church. The woman rested her head against the painting and placed a hand on each side of her face as if to shut out the world.

The boy's mind spun in his skull as he tried to keep his heavy head on his shoulders. He wanted to creep into the church to see his mother but his mind couldn't process how to get back in. He stood a few feet from the entrance. He made his way through the bodies, some with holes or missing limbs, some shielding the holes in their punctured skin or holding onto their nubs with open palms as they screamed for help. Martino spotted the gleam of a gold cross that graced a lady's wrist in the distance.

The boy walked towards the lame arm that laid lifeless on a man's severed leg. He sped up with every stride and hoped to God it wasn't who he knew it was.

"Tino," a deep familiar voice called close to him as thick broad palms grabbed at his sides from behind and lifted and turned the boy.

"Baba," the boy cried as he held onto his father's neck. "I saw a lady over there with a bracelet like mama. It might be her. I need to make sure it's not her."

"You need to make sure nothing," his father roared with an urgency the boy never heard in him before. "You know never to leave the church without me or your mom. You're going home with Aunt Sally."

"No baba just let me…"

The man handed Tino over to his sister who stood silently with her eyes wide to the night. He punched against her soft back and demanded she turn around. He needed to see his mother.

"Everything is fine," she said. "We just need to get home. It's late. You should have been asleep hours ago."

Though young and stupid, Martino knew that nothing that night was fine. He punched and kicked and screamed and cried to go back so that he could see his mother. He did this until he reached his aunt's apartment up the street. There was no use. He was forced under the sheets on his cousin's bed, for his own good he was told.

He knew this was a fight he could not win. He laid on the foreign bed and stared at the tiny ridges on the ceiling and he prayed. He prayed his mother was alright and he'd see her in the morning. He prayed for the people he'd seen pierced and maimed, dying and dead at the front corridor in the church. He prayed they'd live. The dead ones too. And he prayed his tired mind would rest despite the sound and chaos coming from the same block.

A miracle, grace granted him sleep.

~~~

Martino woke a few hours later to a light patter at his door, his head heavier than the night before as if he'd never slept. Memories of the night trickled into his conscious mind. Along with them came the unease of uncertainty he felt but couldn't name.

"Mama," he said as he sat up quick and swift.

"No, it's me," a weak female voice muttered as the door opened. His cousin stood at the door, her eyes dark and tired. The boy knew she must've slept worse than him, if she slept at all. She was short for a girl her age, seventeen she told him a few months ago.

"Dina?" the boy asked as he stood and marched towards her. "Where's mama?"

"Shh," the girl said before he could walk past her out the door.

"I know you want your mom. She's in the hospital now."

"What?" the boy cried.

"She'll be fine," Dina said examining the room with her eyes as if searching for the right words. "Listen, mama and baba are headed out and I have to take care of you. Do you want anything to eat?"

"What happened yesterday?"

"That's not what I-"

"What happened?"

The girl sat herself on her bed next to Tino and wrapped her hand around his shoulder. She smelled like peach shampoo. She must have showered to clean the bloody night off her. Maybe Tino could do the same.

Dina kissed her little cousin on his temple. Tino pushed her away and wiped his wet head. The girl giggled something subtle to herself and looked down at Tino's feet as they swayed to the beat of the boy's unsettled heart.

"There's some bad men out there," she started as she rubbed his shoulder. "They're few but they're strong. They don't like us."

"Why not?"

The girl stopped and stared at her red toe polish shining off her nails. She wriggled and bunched them and let them loose again. Tino saw a tear escape and slide down her pink cheek.

"We're different," she said. "We believe different things."

"So?"

"That's all that matters to some people."

"Who are the bad men?"

"I don't know. Maybe terrorists. Maybe police. Maybe the police are terrorists."

Dina didn't have many words. Tino figured she didn't want to talk because usually she wouldn't stop talking.

"I'm hungry," he said.

"After everything I told you, you're hungry right now?"

"Can you make me something?"

"What do you want to eat?"

"Eggs and liver." Tino hated eggs and liver, but it took a long time to cook.

"Okay, well I have to see if we have any liver. Sit still. If there isn't any I'll at least make you some eggs."

The boy heard his cousin rustle through the pots and pans as she prepared his breakfast. He'd slept in his clothes from the night before, all except his shoes and his white dress shirt stained crimson. His aunt gave him a long sleeved undershirt to wear to sleep instead.

He gently turned the knob and peeked through a small opening between the door and the moulding that surrounded it and saw his cousin across the hall as she reached in the fridge for a piece of liver. The onions frying on the stovetop spat and crackled next to her along with their sweet smell that lingered throughout the apartment. The boy pinched himself through the narrow doorway, closed the bedroom door behind him while his cousin's back was turned, made his way to the front door where he slid into a pair of slippers, and walked out as he closed the door.

The boy knew his mom. She was probably out of the hospital and searching for him by now. She would never leave him alone for too long. He couldn't wait to see her as he marched out of the elevator and onto the street.

Black pickup trucks filled with officers from the Egyptian Shorta sped down the street towards the church. The men on the trucks dressed in all black and covered in padding and patched crests, an emblazoned eagle on their left shoulder, all sported a long jet black gun the length of Tino's body. They rode in silence looking towards the church, their legs spilled through the side windows of the back of the pickup truck. Tino wondered what they were up to. Were they the terrorists that blew up his church and put his mother in the hospital? He spat at the sight of them.

A crowd of teenagers and some older folk marched in front of him in organized chaos. A tall man stood with a giant cross in his hand that hovered a foot above the crowd. A group of others held the same mural of the blood spattered Jesus Tino saw the night before as they marched. They must have peeled it off the church wall. The blood had darkened and dried.

"Mubarak, Mubarak, the heart of the Copts are on fire!" they chanted. Tino spotted a group of protesters in the distance. The rioters stood on one side of the street where the Church of the Two Saints stood, its walls stained red from the night before. Across the street stood Sharq al-Madina mosque. A small patch of black tainted the mosque's cream white walls facing the streets from the explosion the night before. The riot police stood between the two in a large square of officers nine men deep and nine men wide, their black helmets and batons positioned against their shoulders.

A group of teenagers pelted the riot police and the mosque across the street with small stones. Some within the gates of the mosque hurled stones back. One young man in a black t-shirt and curly hair down to his shoulders approached too close to an officer in line, and whipped a stone at the clear shield of the officer's helmet that covered his face. The stone bounced off and the officer jutted towards the teen, grabbed a hold of his arm, pulled him towards the police and brought the baton down against his head with a heavy hand. A fellow officer joined as the rest watched the crowds. Some spat at the boy who cowered at their feet and held his hands above his head and screamed for mercy. A few other protesters tried to help the boy. They were beaten off with batons back into their group.

Tino heard the teen scream. The boy ran fast towards his cry. He felt a pressure pull against his neck from his shirt. The boy fell back on his bottom and looked up behind him.

"Where do you think you're going?" a grizzly voice asked. The boy looked up and saw a bald officer, thick and tall, tower over him. A small group of his comrades stood behind him.

"You're killing him!" Tino cried.

"Don't worry about him," the man said calmly. "Think about yourself. What would happen if you ran up to save him?"

The boy and the officer's stare broke at the sound of a man in the distance.

"Security, are you with us or them?" he yelled above the crowds at the riot police. "You government are all cowards!"

His cries galvanized the protesters who cheered after all his statements.

"Our youth will not stay silent. Our elders will not stay silent. The blood you spilled calls to us from the grave. Cowards! Fight and in time your weapons will fail. God's punishment will come."

Tino noticed another teen in a black t-shirt and black pants a few metres away from the group on one knee. He stood in front of a KFC and faced an empty police truck with a glass bottle in his hand filled with a black liquid. The young man's sight moved between the bottle in his hand and the police who faced the other way to watch the man with the megaphone hurl insults at them. He took a handkerchief out of his back pocket, dipped it into the black liquid in his bottle, took it out and lit it. He stuffed the kerchief in the bottle, corked it, and whipped it into the open back window of the police truck towards the driver's seat before he ran back and disappeared between the crowds.

The bottle smashed against the truck and lit its inside. The bald officer that pulled Tino to the ground spotted the burning truck, cursed the black day and ran towards the vehicle with his comrades. The boy watched him call for firefighters on his walkie-talkie as he ran. The bald officer turned back and yelled at one of his men to grab the boy, just in case. A tall lanky officer turned back and held the boy with one hand from the back of his neck, his other hand pulling at the boy's collar. Tino sat so lost in the flames, he barely noticed.

He examined the fire as it grew, the crowd gathering around the burning truck and jeering, the flame fueled by the fear of the men with shields. It grew and ate at the truck flicker by flicker, flame by flame, until it spilled out of the open windows as the dangling legs of the officers did just minutes before, and consumed the truck whole. He felt it's heavy heat warm him, breathe life into his small frame. The boy, still terrified his mother might not be well, identified with the fire. It's rage. It's relentless destruction of everything evil. He sat between a ruthless fire and the cold bare fingers of the law digging into his neck and wondered the difference.

A firetruck approach the blaze, its siren cutting through the chaos of sound that littered the open air. Firefighters jumped out of the truck and pulled out a thick beige hose from the back. They assembled the hose, connected it to a water line and pointed it towards the burning truck. It's stream of water slowly subdued the flames. Within a few minutes, the fire was out. But not before it got its way.

The plastic shell that covered the pickup's back had melted and collapsed in on itself. Patches of black paint congealed and mixed with blotches of grey and a dusty white on the car's body. The tires flattened, melted and conformed to the shape of the steel they circled. The fire relented against the stream of water that choked its life only after it destroyed what it needed to. And the big dumb face of Colonel Sanders painted on a short building looked on from the other side of the street and smiled. Tino noticed the colonel, how he watched in amusement as the car burned, and he laughed.

The officer that held the boy's neck was called on his walkie-talkie towards the protesters who grew aggressive in their faceoff with the police blockade.

"You're lucky," he said as he let go and ran off towards his comrades.

"Tino!" a frantic voice called behind him. He didn't have time to run. A small thin hand grabbed him by his arm and turned him around. Dina found him. She marched him hand on wrist back to her apartment and scolded him as she walked.

She cried. Tino knew he scared her by disappearing. But he had not yet found his mom. He tried to wriggle out of her hold but the boy only wasted his energy. Her grip was too tight, his wrist hurt. He stepped away from her towards the church but she pulled at him, picked him up in her arms and marched home as fast as she could.

They got to her home in a few minutes. She forced him into her room, closed the door, and sat inside with the boy, her back against the door. She pulled him down to the floor with her.

"What are you doing?" the boy cried as he tried to push Dina over and reach for the knob. "I need to find mama."

Dina wrestled the boy down and held his hands still to his sides and told him repeatedly to relax. After much resistance, the boy realized there wasn't much he could do. He buried his face in his palms.

"I want watermelon," the boy said.

"Do you think I'm falling for that again?"

"Not you. I want mama to cut me watermelon. I'm so hungry."

Dina let out a deep breath and wiped her wet eyes.

"I have something to tell you," she said. She sounded resigned from her words, trying to distance herself from them.

Tino didn't like the sound of her voice. He didn't want to hear it.

"I want mama. And I want watermelon."

"Tino, habibi. I lied. Your mom didn't make it."

The boy turned to his cousin and stared.

"Make it where?"

"Like giddu," Dina said. "She's with giddu now."

The boy's mind went blank. He sat and stared at the old drawer in front of him. An empty lightness grew in the pit of his stomach and travelled throughout his body down to the tips of his toes and up to his head. He tried to process his cousin's words but they felt flimsy in the mind of an eight year old. It felt as if the words spilled out of her mouth and shattered on the tiled floor around him, their crystal shards digging deeper into his skin the more he moved. So he sat still.

"Tino?"

He barely noticed his cousin calling him.

"Tino you're not talking." She put her arm around the boy and held him close. That touch. The warmth. The softness of her cheek against his. Like his mother. But she was not her mother.

The shards had dug too deep.

He stood up, turned to Dina and clenched his fat, tiny fists, and swung. Tino knocked her in the nose. His wild fists came from all angles down on her head and body. She shielded her face with one arm and grabbed at the boy with the other. The girl tried to stand but Tino knocked her over. He felt the heat on his face and the hurt in his fists. He kicked at Dina as she tried to wrestle him back down to the floor. She managed to clench both his arms to his back and push him to the ground face down. The boy screamed as his cheek rested on the ceramic floor in the damp wet heat of his own saliva.

"I'm so sorry," Dina wept as the weight of her knee pinned the boy to the ground.

A knock came from the front door accompanied by the jangle of keys.

"Tino," his father called as he entered. He sounded very tired. Dina lifted her knee off the boy's back and ran out of the room before he could stand. Tino followed close behind. He saw his father in the living room next to his Aunt Sally. The man's eyelids drooped and darkened by the weight of a long night. A faint stubble speckled his tired face. He wore the same clothes from the night before.

"Time to go home," he said.

Tino walked away from his cousin and aunt and father and out of the open door into the hall. His father followed him. They made their way to the car and stepped in.

A cloud of silence hovered above them.

"Mama died," his father said.

Tino said nothing.

~~~

His mother's funeral was held at night. Tino and his father travelled to the Monastery of St. Mina thirty kilometres west. Thousands of people dressed in black filled the church and spilled through the doors and onto the front steps to attend the funeral. Tino and his father sat three rows from the front as family of the martyrs. He watched the procession of caskets above men's shoulders weave through the crowds as the people reached their hands to touch the wood and pray for the blessing of their churches newest saints. Tino didn't look too long at each casket. He didn't want to read his mother's name on the side. He didn't want to know which one she laid in. The thought of her body, mouth closed and dead eyes opened to infinity, knotted the boy's bowels so tight he wanted to vomit.

Twenty three caskets laid at the front of the altar. The priests prayed a sombre chant and begged God to open up the doors of paradise. The crowds wailed and wept. Tino sat amongst them alone in his thoughts. He wished they would shut up.

A girl his age sat next to him in a black dress. Brown skin. Black eyes and short legs that dangled above the pews. She cried. Her father sat next to her with his face to the red carpet.

"Who died?" he whispered to the girl.

"My mother," she said wiping her tears.

"Me too."

"I'm sorry."

"Can you stop crying?"

"My mother died."

"But you need to stop crying. You look weak and stupid," the boy whispered.

The girl rubbed her tears and sniffed.

"You're a horrible person," she hushed. She slid off the pew and sat at her father's other side. The man raised his head from the ground, slid towards Tino and lowered his head again.

Tino looked up at his own father. He sat facing the altar where his dead wife laid in a box and stared with hard narrow eyes and a stiff jaw like steel. His father always looked that way. But there was a glint in his eyes that the boy read as fear or rage or both. He couldn't tell.

Tino and his father took the bus back to the city after the funeral. Neither cared to stay for long for the condolences.

"You know, after they killed St. Mina," his father said as they sat and stared out the window and watched the night horizon stretch darkness to the ends of the world, "an angel visited the pope and told him to take the saint's body to the Western Dessert. The pope told St. Mina's sister, and she put his body on a camel and they rode through the outskirts of Alexandria. Then the camel stopped. And it wouldn't move anymore."

"Where did it stop?"

"Right where that church is," his dad said pointing to the church as it shrunk into itself as they pulled away. "His sister knew the camel wouldn't move for a reason."

"Why did God want his body somewhere other than where he died?"

"Well. Sometimes, even in death you have to move. Maybe you have purpose somewhere else."

"But why did the camel stop right there? What's so special about this dessert that God wanted St. Mina's body here?"

The man looked off to the side and turned towards the front. He sat back and reclined his seat and rested his head against its back.

"I don't know," his father said. "God does a lot of things I don't understand."

The boy didn't ask any more questions. He rested his head against the window and closed his eyes. He'd be in a new country within a week. Away from his family. Away from his old friends and his community. Away from his mother's body. The knot in his stomach tightened, and he slept under the blanket of his own fear.

~~~

Tino sat next to the window on the plane, his father to his right on the aisle seat. He'd never been in a plane before though he'd seen them fly above him all the time. Up close, his plane looked like a huge tin bird. The inside was packed with people and hot, much like Egypt herself. The boy rubbed his sweaty palms on his pants and imagined his new life in Canada. His angel would save him from the snow bears. His mother promised him. But then she told him she would sit next to him on the plane to Canada. The boy shook the memory off.

The flight attendants went through the pre-flight cautions and ensured all the people on board had their seatbelts fastened. Within a few minutes the plane rolled off the tarmac and onto the runway.

The plane rushed down the uneven concrete increasing its speed with distance. Tino felt the tires bump and roll like thunder beneath him. He forced his quick breath to slow and clutched his armrest as the plane lifted its nose and moved from earth to sky. The boy felt his insides drop to his seat as the engine's pitch heightened with the plane. His ears plugged as if filled with water and the sound of the vertical world around him descended. He opened and closed his mouth a few times until his ears popped and the tone of the world around him came back.

He stared outside at the wide barren land of no fruits. Huge patches of dessert swallowed much of the Alexandrian landscape and the streets that cut through and the square patches of grass and the sea green that faded into dark blue of the Mediterranean and the tiny people that shrunk with the plane's ascension sat low before the boy well below his feet and he smiled. The land of bad men and dark blood and dead bodies that had taken everything away stayed in its place as he flew away. Far away.

The boy spotted a white dove below him as the plane approached its peak. His mother told him to say a prayer every time he'd see a bird in the sky. Birds carried prayers to heaven his mother said. The birds sing your prayers to God at his gates she said.

Tino closed his eyes and clasped his hands and bowed his head. *Let me see her one more time.*

~~~

Twelve hours in the sky among the clouds and the boy saw the world like a place he'd never known. The clouds looked different from above. Opaque but fragile as if they could dissolve by touch like cotton candy. The waters below stretched to the ends of the Earth and rippled under the huge sun perched against a blank backdrop of nothing, undefined in its shape and piercing in its gaze. Its reflection shimmered atop the uneasy water where the universe held the Earth stitched to its seams.

The boy wondered how far he'd have to travel if he wanted to get to heaven. How far and how high and for how long would the plane need to fly if he were to reach his mother in time and space. He knew she watched him. There was an implied promise between them that she'd always be with him. Those unspoken words he felt in himself good and true.

~~~

At the end of the infinite waters the boy spotted shore and white cut into squares of land as the plane descended. Within an hour, a voice from the intercom cut through the boy's dreams and announced the aircraft now hovered over Toronto and would be landing shortly. His body felt weightless with the planes decline. His father pointed to the land below them.

"That's our new home," he said.

"Wow."

"See that tall tower with the needle? I think that's the CN Tower. One of the biggest in the world."

"The pointy one?"

"Yes. And those huge white blankets, that's snow. I've never seen it before either. Except on television."

The streets severed the snow into sections. The boy was eager to run his hands through the snow. He imagined it felt like ice cream. Solid and slippery and possibly delicious. His mother loved ice cream too.

Landing was rougher then takeoff. The airplane rolled onto the tarmac and connected its front door to the jetway that lead into the airport. The captain welcomed the passengers to Canada and wished them safe travels. A flight attendant stood at the front of the plane motioning instructions on how to exit the plane dictated by a recorded message played over the intercom. The front doors beside her opened. Tino felt a cold draft breeze through the cabin. He chattered his teeth and held his arms close to his body. He wished he'd worn a jacket, but none of the jackets he owned could protect him against a cold so dense. And the cold only grew as he walked off the plane with his dad and into the jetway. The boy saw his father shudder.

"Nothing like this in Egypt," he said.

"Is it like this forever?"

"I hope to God it isn't."

The two got off the plane in line and marched through the jetway and into Pearson International where the heat kicked in and Tino grew warm again. The boy and his father followed the crowds as they moved through long corridors. Tino looked up and all around him. Half the ceiling hovered as bare glass above him and he stared into the sky he'd just inhabited, blue and wide and free. There were no glass ceilings in Alexandria.

The floors were tiled white and grey and clean. Walking through the corridors, the boy spotted old white people with eyes as blue as his mother's. They smiled at him as they approached. He looked away. There were black people darker then the Nubians he'd seen in Aswan, and narrow-eyed Asians and smooth haired brown people and men with earrings and long hair and women with short hair and pantsuits and all kinds of colours and dresses the boy had never seen.

"Baba," the boy said. "Why is that man wearing an earring?"

"He's confused."

The two made their way through customs and got their bags from the baggage carousel at the end of the airport and waited by the carousel for his uncle John who picked them up within the hour. His car was sleek and black and brand new. A Mercedes.

"I like your car, uncle," the boy said.

"Not bad eh? I worked hard for her."

The man was a pharmacist and owned three pharmacies in the area.

"You can do anything you want in this country if you work hard enough," he said.

The boy ran his fingers through the stitching in the leather on his seat. He pressed a button and watched the car window roll down. The cold seeped in through the narrow opening and the boy rushed to close it.

"By the way," uncle John said. "I'm sorry about the-"

"Don't mention it," his father said.

"Were you talking about mama?" the boy said.

"Yeah son. I'm really sorry about what happened. I'm sure it must be-"

"Shut up," the boy said with a hush as cold as the new country.

"Tino, apologize," his dad growled. "I'll take off my shoe."

"Do it," the boy said, surprised at his own words. "But he's not allowed to talk about mama like she's dead."

His dad's face wrinkled and his eyes narrowed and he looked back at the boy and sprung his arm at him. John stretched his right arm towards Tino's father and blocked him.

"Whoa, listen Karim it's okay," he said and lowered his voice. "Look at everything that happened. How's he supposed to be okay?"

His father turned towards the streets and stared at his boy through the rearview mirror and calmed his voice.

"Watch what you say boy."

"I'm sorry if I said the wrong thing Tino," his uncle said.

They arrived at the lowrise building owned by St. Mary's Coptic Church in Mississauga who sponsored them. His father and uncle grabbed their luggage and took Tino to the seventh floor to a small white-walled apartment at the end of the hall. His father shook hands with John and thanked him for all his help. He closed the door and took off his shoe. Tino ran to the bathroom and closed the door and tried to lock it behind him. His father forced the door open. He grabbed the boy by the wrist, held him against the wall and swung his shoe at the boy's left side. Tino cried and blocked his body with his hand, sliding down to the floor. His father held the boy's wrist behind his back and swiped a few more swings at the boy's flank.

The man stood up straight with his shoe in his right hand and breathed deep from the short run through the house and the work he did to pin his son down. He looked down at the boy who stared down at the tiles. Tino wiped the tears from his eyes and held his left side, red and hot to the touch in his palm.

"I know it's been difficult," his father said. "It's been hard on everyone. I miss her too. But I will not tolerate you talking to my brother like that."

He walked out of the bathroom to unpack his shisha. Tino turned to touch his red skin onto the cold ceramic tiles and sobbed softly. He laid on the floor and remembered the times his mother stood between the boy and his dad, calming her husband with cool words and a light touch.

A FACE LIKE THE MOON

~~~

Tino and his father walked to the bus stop on a cold mid-January morning, the boy's body snug in a thick red winter coat and black snow pants and a scarf and mittens and a Maple Leafs toque. Thirty dollars all in for everything from Value Village, down from fifty after haggling. The boy strode through the snow with his mittened hand in his father's. His body felt warm and his face cold and numb and leaking from the nose.

Tino tried to pull his hand away from his father's but he wouldn't let go. The snow glowed perfect white under the light of the sun and worked to shades of brown as it approached the snowbanks on the side of the street. A large truck with a scoop the width of its face shoveled snow to the side of the street and sprinkled something that looked like specks of glass underneath its path.

"What is that?" the boy asked.

"I think it's salt. It melts the snow."

"That's too big to be salt."

The cold breeze bit at the bare skin on his neck. He stretched his scarf to cover the skin and wrapped it tight around his neck.

It was Tino's first day of school in Canada. He sat alone at the front of the bus across from a tiny olive skinned girl in pigtails with bright pink Hello Kitty earmuffs. She swayed her legs and stared at him as he watched the cars outside his window. He felt her stare at the back of his neck.

"Hi," she squeaked.

The boy turned and looked at her. She wore a short innocent smile and a jacket as puffy as the boy's. Her arms hovered a few inches between her waist pushed away from the padding in her sleeves.

"What is your name?" she said.

"*Martino.*"

"I never seen you before," she said.

"*Zis is my ferrest day*," he said slow, listening to the sound of his words. He knew enough English to get by from his private school back in Alexandria.

"You speak very funny."

The boy scowled at the girl and blew her a raspberry. She giggled and pulled her dangling legs up towards her body and held her boots in her hands.

"You're not from here," she said.

The boy turned away and back to the streets.

"Where are you from?" she asked.

Tino didn't answer.

"Boy!" she said. "Where are you from? Why did you turn from me?"

If he didn't answer, she might keep asking.

"I am from Egypt," he said.

"Really? Wow! I'm from Syria," she said in Arabic. The boy had some trouble with her Syrian dialect, though he understood it better than English.

"I don't like your Arabic," he said in his own dialect. "All of you Syrians' sound like girls."

"I am a girl!" she said and readjusted her legs.

The boy nodded.

"Do you like snow?" she asked.

"No."

"Why not?"

"It's cold."

"That means you don't know how to play with it," she said. "Come with me at recess and we can build a snowman and we can name him Martino like your name. And we can make a snow girl too and we can name her Christina like my name and they can get married."

The boy tried to fight back a weak smirk.

"What's a snowman?"

"I'll show you," the girl said.

He looked at her, examined her round brown eyes and tiny

hands in pink mitts and straight brown hair and that short staccato smile. He smiled back and nodded.

They reached school together. The bell rang and Tino followed the girl through the gate and to the playground, past the yard to the front doors. He got in line behind the girl and waited until a thin lady in a long brown ponytail called the line in and walked them to class. She watched the boy as he put his jacket and backpack and scarf and mitts on the rack and made his way into class. The lady waved the boy towards her and bent down to meet his eyes.

"Hi," she smiled. "My name is Mrs. Riley. I'm your third grade teacher. You must be Martino."

The boy nodded.

"You look very sophisticated in that sweater vest Martino. Who picked it out for you?"

"*Baba bought it for me from Valu Vellaj,*" the boy said.

"What a cute little accent you have. Where is that from?"

"*Egypt.*"

"Wow! We have pharaoh in our class," she said. "Well, usually when we have a new student, we get him to introduce himself to the class. Would you be comfortable saying a few words to the class about yourself? Your name, where you're from, what you like doing. Anything."

The boy shook his head.

"No? Not even a few words? It's scary I know, but it will help you make friends quicker if the kids get to know you right?"

Tino shrugged. The woman spoke too fast for him to understand.

"Just give it a try," she said as she grabbed his hand and led him inside. She stood him beside her desk and quieted the class. She told everyone of the new student and asked the boy to introduce himself.

"*Hi I am Martino. I am fine how are you?*"

"Hi Martino," the class said.

"Tell us about yourself Martino. Where you're from, what you like to do in your spare time."

"I am from Egypt. I like to play toy cars."

"His English is stupid," a chubby Asian boy in the front of the class yelled. The class laughed. Tino felt his cheeks warm and redden.

"James!" Mrs. Riley said. "Any more of that and you're in with me for recess." James slunk back into his seat.

Mrs. Riley thanked Tino for his introduction and patted his back. She told him to find a seat in the class where he was comfortable. Tino grabbed a chair off a short stack and placed it beside Christina at a small hexagonal table.

He sat next to her for the morning and listened to Mrs. Riley as she explained counting by twos to the class. He didn't understand much of what she said and he didn't count along with the class when they practiced. He sat back and pretended to absorb the information.

Mrs. Riley gave free time at the end of the period before recess. The boy picked up a Lego set from the front of the class. He built a small fort out of yellow and brown Lego pieces. Christina helped him by arranging the Lego men and women at a table in the fort.

"They're drinking orange juice," the girl said.

The bell rang.

Christina grabbed the boy's hand and pulled him to the coat rack outside. The two dressed in their winter wear and ran outside with the other children. Christina led him through the yard towards the thickest snow that climbed up to the boy's knees. She took a handful of the white powder and patted it into a small ball.

The boy stood and stared eyes wide at the novel substance. He took off his mitts and pressed and rolled his own ball of snow. Scattered and fragile as it was, it hardened the more he squeezed until it solidified in his hands, the cold piercing his skin. He dropped the snowball onto the ground below him and put on his mitts.

The girl flashed a smile at Tino and rolled the little snowball across the ground. The boy helped and saw the snowball grow thick and heavy. When they were done, the once tiny snowball had grown to reach up to Tino's waist.

"Now we make another," she said.

The second was smaller, only up to his knees, but still heavy. And a third even smaller, about the size of the boy's head. Christina asked Tino to help her put the second ball on top of the larger one. He and Christina pushed the second snowball against the first and rolled it upwards until it perched on the thick base. She went and grabbed the smallest snowball and placed it at the top.

She told Tino to find a stick on the boundary of the forest south of the yard. They picked up a handful and created arms and a mouth. Christina poked eyes out of the top snowball with her hooded finger. She slid her earmuffs off her head and placed them on the bald head of the figure and her pink mitts on its frail wooden hands. She reached into a pocket below her jacket in her pants and pulled out a pencil. She jammed it below and beneath its eyes, eraser side out, and the boy saw the bare white man for the first time. He stared at Tino and smiled a scraggly wooden smile. The girl stepped back and stood beside Tino and stared at the life they'd created. They boy felt the silence between them. He felt that it was good.

"We built this thing," she said.

She grabbed his thick hooded head in her mitted palms and pulled him towards her and kissed his cheek like his mother used to. He felt a warmth move through his body amongst the cold.

"Eeeeaarthquaaaaaake!" a voice cried in the distance as it got louder and crashed into the snowman's round form. The Asian boy that laughed at Tino in class blitzed the structure with his body and tackled the middle ball pushing it to the ground where it smashed into dull undefined pieces along with the head. James the Asian and the few boys behind him laughed.

"Why did you do that to him? I loved him." Christina whimpered.

"That's what happens when a girl kisses you," James said as he turned to Tino. "Your snowman dies of AIDS."

The warmth that had spread through Tino's body turned cold and he could feel the greyness of day around him. He scowled and marched towards the narrow-eyed boy that laughed at the sight of the destruction of the broken man Tino made with Christina. Tino took off his mitts and wound his heavy arm back and swung his tiny fist at the Asian and knocked the tip of his nose.

James fell to the ground and held his face and cried. His friends gasped and shoved Tino as he knelt at James' feet. Tino pushed the other boys off him and took off his boot, held the toe in his palm and came down on the submitted boy's head. James wailed. He covered his eyes and nose and lips with his palms and the sight of his fear pushed the boy's anger and the boot came down harder again.

"Stop," James cried, his words loud and raw. "I'm sorry!"

Tino beat his face with the boot until James' blood drained from his nose and dyed the snow red. The sight of it justified Tino.

"What's happening?" an approaching voice called. Tino looked up and saw Mrs. Riley trudge quick through the snow.

"Martino, up!" she said. She grabbed James by the shoulder and helped him to his feet. His nose was red and blood smeared across his face and on his gloves, down below his lips to his chin where it dried.

Tino forced his heavy head up. He held his mouth agape and stared at the boot in his hand. The bloody face. The crimson snow. He breathed and felt his mind sober. The sight of blood reminded him of the streets of Alexandria on that warm winter night. The memory of his mother's hand risen above the bodies, lifeless and limp but still capable to grasp the boy's mind, latch itself to the back of his scalp, its fingers dug between his thick black hair grasped at his skin. Escaping to the new country couldn't erase the memory of old blood.

"You need to come with me," Mrs. Riley said as she grabbed his wrist and pulled him towards the school. "You too James."

Martino made it seven steps before he stopped, bent at his waist, and vomited what little was left in his stomach.

~~~

Tino and James sat on separate sides of the same room waiting for their parents. Tino ran his eyes through the narrow lines that separated the grey tiles on the floor like the streets that severed snow and land he saw from the sky staring down at the new city and he remembered his dad pointing out the places and scenery and he wondered what his dad would do when he found out what happened.

A short Asian man in uniform entered the school from the front doors, his hair slicked back and face sleek and edged and his eyes narrow and terrible. The principal greeted the officer at the door. James ran to him and hugged his waist and cried, his face now cleaned of blood and a reddened tissue clogging his left nostril.

The principal led the man out into the entrance and explained to him what had happened, the officer all the while dodged his eyes between her and Tino through the large glass part of the wall that separated the corridor from the office.

"I assure you," Tino heard the principal say behind the wall. "He will be punished."

The officer asked repeatedly if he could speak to Tino for just a minute, his voice jagged but calm. The principal told him that was against school policy. After much trying, the officer nodded his goodbye to the principal and walked out with his hand on his boy's head.

Within the minute, Tino spotted his father walk in and say hello to the principal. He marched up to his son and set his eyes on Tino's. Tino withdrew his cold stare and glared back down at the tiles. The principal explained what had happened to his father.

"I don't know how it is in your country," she said. "But in Canada, this behaviour is unacceptable." The boy would not be permitted to return to school for another week. The father stood and nodded. The principal handed Tino a paper that she told him explains his suspension. He folded the sheet and slid it in his pocket.

"*Okay*," his father said. "*I will deal wiz him when we get home.*"

The father motioned the boy up when the principal finished, said goodbye, and the boy and his father made their way outside.

"I know this is a bad time," his father said. "But I have a surprise for you."

The man walked the boy away from the bus station and towards the parking lot. They stopped at a large white station wagon with no curves. Straight lines all around with a star on its front grill. Long panels of fake wood stretched across its side. Patches of rust ate at the body from all corners. Tino's father unlocked the passenger door and carried the boy up to the seat and strapped him. The cloth that lined the roof had separated and hung off the topmount steel right above the boy's head.

"It's a Dodge," the man said without a hint of gruff in his voice. Still, the boy knew it would come.

"Dodge Aries."

"I like it," the boy said, making sure not to say too much.

His father turned the key in the ignition. The boy heard the engine squelch for breath until it caught power and roared awake with an uneven rumble.

"She needs a little bit of love, but she works," his dad said.

The boy nodded. A silence fell between them.

Tino heard the dull moan of the tires every time his father turned the wheel. He examined the fake wood panels that ran across the dash intersected by old metal knobs that controlled the radio and volume and air conditioning and heat. The car smelled like cigarette smoke. He felt every bump and pothole in the road. He spotted a lighter in a narrow cubby underneath the air conditioner. His dad probably bought one for his shisha.

"You know this is not Egypt. You can't be beating people you don't agree with in this country," his father said, his words angrier then his tone.

"I know. I'm sorry."

"So you beat him pretty good huh?"

Tino looked over at his dad who sat with his cheeks bunched suppressing a smile.

"Yeah."

"With your boot."

"Yes."

"And he cried?"

"Yes."

The man chuckled.

"That's horrible. Next time something bad happens, I want you to tell the teacher."

The boy scratched his head.

"You don't sound like you care," he said.

"I have to care."

"Why?"

"Because your mom would've cared."

Tino shut his eyes at his father's words and leaned back. He pulled his hat down to cover his ears and thought of Christina.

"She used to be so annoying with her morality, that woman. Did she ever tell you how we met?"

The boy shook his head.

"We met at a church soup kitchen. St. John the Compassionate. I didn't wanna be there but I was fresh out of university and mama needed to get me married. She said there were some pretty girls there and they were good girls. I went so she would get off my case. And I saw Yasmine there. She was sitting with some homeless folk, eating and talking with them. And I saw those blue eyes Tino and I'm telling you, I was in love. I had to sit at that table, I had no choice. I just wanted to look at her a little. So I smiled and introduced myself. Pulled up a seat across from her between a fat guy and a skinny guy. They both smelled like garbage. And there I was faking a smile and talking to these people like they meant something to me, waiting for her to jump in so I could talk to her a little. But she barely talked. All she did was eat and smile and listen.

"So the guy beside me, the fat guy. I guess he believed my act because he started opening up to me. Told me he once had a wife and kids. They talk when they think you care, those people. He was an engineer apparently. Doing pretty good in life. Until one day he comes home early. Opens up the door to his bedroom and sees his wife on the bed with a blanket over her naked body, and another man running towards the closet. I think the fat man picked up a book or something and attacked the other guy, but the other guy was too big and he beat him unconscious. He woke up on his back. His wife had taken the baby and ran. He never saw her or his child again. Hit the bottle hard and lost everything.

"Anyway, so he's telling that story, and I look over at your mom, her eyes wide and blue, and she stared at the man and just sat there. A fork in her hand. Said nothing. I couldn't tell what she was thinking. He wasn't looking at her. He never took his eyes off his food."

Tino's father's face sobered and straightened and stared at the road like he was watching the broken lines of his life pass underneath him. All he could do was keep moving.

"And then she speaks. I'll never forget her words."

"What did she say?"

"She said, 'I'll pray you see your kid again.'"

"That's it?"

"That's all she needed to say. That fat man blubbered like a baby at her words. He tried to hide it by eating his food as he cried. At the time, I thought he looked so stupid. Like a sad grazing hippo."

The man laughed.

"But you know, I got to thinking. Any woman who could sit down with the dirtiest people, eat with them despite their smell, talk to them and call them friends. Any woman who could see the humanity in a person that everyone else sees as trash, there's something special about that woman. I knew I needed to get to know her. And we got married," his father said and slapped his knee and smiled.

The boy held his head over his lap.

"She loved people," his father said. "She loved you most of all."

Tino held his tears, not daring to wink. He picked up his dad's lighter from the cubby and flicked at the sparkwheel and pushed down on the fork trying to distract himself from the memory of a past life that swore to destroy him if he lost himself in it.

The lighter spat sparks that died on birth. He tried many times but a flame wouldn't catch. Strange. He'd seen his father do it a million times. It looked so easy when he did, but it wouldn't work for Tino.

"You gotta press hard and fast," his dad said.

"I'm trying."

"Come on boy. You've seen me do it a million times. How are you gonna light up a shisha for me when I'm old and dying?"

The boy spotted red and blue alternating lights in his sideview mirror. A cop car pulled from behind him to the left lane next to his father. The officer rolled down his window. James's father smiled and waved and pointed to the side of the road. Tino's father breathed, shook his head and pulled to the shoulder and stopped.

The officer parked behind the boy and his father. He stepped out of the vehicle and approached the driver's side with a smooth clean step. Tino's father rolled down his window.

"Constable Wang, Peel Regional Police," the officer said pointing to his nametag on his coat. "License and registration."

"*Yes ser,*" his father said and pulled out the registration for his car and his international driver's license.

The officer checked the articles handed to him.

"International eh? Where are you from?"

"*I am Egyptian ser.*"

"Oh, Egypt wow. Guess I should make sure I don't make any sudden moves eh? Make sure I don't get blown up," the officer smirked.

Tino winced.

"*No ser of course not. I don't blow up anysing.*"

"You know why I stopped you?"

"*No ser.*"

"One of your taillights is out."

"*I don't sink so. I bought zis car today and-*"

"See you people don't listen. I'm telling you your taillight is out. What is it with you sand niggers? Why can't you ever co-operate?" the officer smiled with that cold jagged tone he'd heard him use in the principal's office.

"*You call me negger?*"

"What are you people if you aren't sand niggers?"

"*Listen to me small eye-*"

The officer pulled his baton from out of his holster and hit it hard against the ridge of Tino's father's open window.

"I'm sorry, did you just call me small eye?"

"*Yes because you call me-*"

"We have rules in this country you know? What you just said, that's a hate crime. You're not allowed to be talking about me and my ethnicity in derogatory terms like that. I can write you up right now you know? You'll have to go to court. Maybe spend a few days in jail. Pay a big fine to this fine country. Is that what you want? You and your violent little nigger son?"

Tino's dad contorted his lips and cracked his neck. He breathed and looked down at his son, back to the officer. He rested his head against his seat and stared at the still broken lines that laid on the asphalt to his side. The boy had never seen his father back off from another man before.

"I asked is that what you want?"

"*No ser.*"

"You're a sand nigger right? I want you to admit what you are so we can move forward. Are you a sand nigger?"

Tino's father breathed in.

"Are you a sand nigger?"

"*Yes ser.*"

"Say it."

"*Say what?*"

"Say I am a sand nigger."

"*No please ser-*"

"I'm sorry, did you want me to refer you to the courts for your hate crime?"

Tino's father closed his eyes.

"*I am a sand negger,*" he mumbled.

"I'm sorry? I didn't hear you. Say it louder. I am a dirty sand nigger."

"*I am a sand negger,*" his father raised his voice.

"Say it louder," the officer commanded. "I can barely hear you."

"*I am a sand negger!*" Tino's father yelled and sliced the air with his open palms. "*I am a dirty sand negger! Is zis what you wanted? I am a sand negger!*"

"Sir you're becoming belligerent. I'm gonna have to ask you to step out of the car." The officer stepped back and fingered his gun on his holster. He continued to demand Tino's father step out. He did as the officer said, spitting curses at him in Arabic.

Tino thought the officer spoke to him as well so he stepped out from the passenger door. He saw the officer push his father up against the car and reach for his cuffs. Tino panicked and wished he could help. He had no one else if his father left. Tino flicked at the sparkwheel on his lighter incessantly in fear and wondered how he could help him.

The lighter caught flame amongst the cold around him. The

flame danced against the breeze, dipping and rising in protest of the cold. Tino stood for a moment mesmerized by the power he held in his tiny hands.

Restorer of order among chaos. The boy grabbed the suspension form the principal had given him from his pocket and walked towards the police car, it's passenger window still open. He touched the swaying flame to the tip of the paper and watched it catch fire. The boy felt his heart knock against his ribcage. He tossed the sheet into the front of the cop car.

The officer caught hold of his handcuffs, jammed his shoulder into Tino's father's back and raised the cuffs above the man's struggling wrists. Tino jumped towards his father and kicked the officer in his shin. He screamed and dropped the cuffs to the floor. Tino ran away from his car and the officer chased him. The boy was fast for a child his age and slipped between Wang's fingers. A hundred metres out and Wang caught him by the hood and threw him to the ground. Tino scooped a palmful of snow and tossed it at Wang's face.

"*Officer*," Tino's father yelled from a short distance. "*Your car is on fire!*" he smiled.

Wang stood up and turned around. The flame had grown and consumed the front and back seats of the vehicle. The flame licked at the air to the side of the open window, stealing space across the grey skyline and lighting the dull afternoon alive.

Wang stood up and stared mouth agape at the sight before him. There it was. Justice for its keeper. Chaos for the promoter of order. Destruction of the crooked foundation that became law and an invitation to rebuild from the bottom up. More than destruction, this was art. This was truth.

Eat, fire. Eat. Eat the steel and bend it to its shell. Eat the plastic lights that flashed and followed so many men before. Eat the cop. Eat his pride. Eat his dirty smile, his small eyes and narrow vision. Eat his dignity.

I did what I could mama.

A FACE LIKE THE MOON

On a hot day in the village of Koshk in the furthest south, Morqos stood in a cornfield stocking ears of corn with his father under a hanging sun, its light fading into the clouds. The boy, not yet ten, wiped the sweat from his brow on his sleeve and looked over at his father.

His father was a furry man, hairy everywhere except the crown of his head. A large sweat stain spread from his collar bone down his back as the hours passed. At midday, Morqos saw that his father's movements slowed, became more cautious as he worked. His face dripped and his head hung low. His breaths grew heavy and short, though he tried to hide his weakness from his son.

"Hot day," he muttered to Morqos.

The boy looked up at his father and nodded as he peeled the skin off an ear of corn.

"And they say tomorrow's gonna be worse. Can you believe that?"

Morqos rubbed his palm on his closed eye and shrugged.

"What's a matter with you boy?" his father asked. "You need to speak. People call me father of the dumb boy because you barely speak a word."

The boy opened up his sack and threw a piece of corn in. His father's words were too dull, too tired. He'd heard them so many times before. Still, the boy hated disappointing him.

"It's hot," Morqos said. "And I'm thirsty."

His father coughed and rubbed a cloth from his pocket to his face.

"Me too," he said pointing at the wooden gate. A tin bucket sat beneath it. "Go get water. Go quick," he mumbled. "The quicker you come, the more corn we pick."

Morqos was waiting for him to ask. He ran to the gate, picked up the bucket and marched towards the well at the north side of the village. The well lay between Koshk and Abu-Sandal, the neighbouring village. Morqos used to go all the time with his mother in better days.

The boy knew his father would be angry if he took long, so he paced, swinging his bucket from side to side, and watched the clouds move towards the end of the world. He wondered how far they fell when they reached the tip. He imagined the clouds smashing into so many pieces as they hit the ground, slivers of white and fluff everywhere.

Can clouds smash into slivers? Morqos had to rethink the scene after realizing puffy things couldn't be shattered. Maybe they dented. That made more sense – round things dent. Like the head of Morqos' baby brother when his young cousin dropped the boy. Morqos found it strange that the only thing that could stop his brother's crying was the event that killed him.

He remembered his mother screaming something from the mouth of an injured donkey, pushing her niece off her little boy, and crying and praying, begging God he could breathe. Morqos ran towards her and peered over her shoulder at his baby brother's smashed head. He looked almost the same as before the fall, but now he was deformed. His face lost all movement. The little boy's dead eyes looked above him at the ceiling as if he saw through it. Morqos wanted to help him, tried to reach for the dent in his head. His mother pushed him off before he got close. Cuddling the boy at her breast didn't bring him back to life. His cousin ran out of the house as quick as she could with wet eyes.

Morqos didn't know his brother well. He might have even hated him when he was alive, he wasn't sure. But he worked hard to hold his tears in that day. He walked out of his shack and towards the clothesline where a wet towel hung to dry. He unclipped the towel, rested his back against the wall of his home, and slid down to the ground with the towel over his head. He sat and breathed in. He didn't talk much after that day.

Before the accident, his mother used to walk to the well with him all the time. He missed the mother who once taught him. She disappeared into the turquoise walls in his shack after the accident, no more present then the chair she sat on as she worked and prayed and cried.

Morqos spotted the well in the distance. Grey and made of jagged flat stones plastered together, it stood three feet above the ground – slightly shorter than the boy himself. A hook hung on a rope connected to a pulley swung gently in the wind above the well. Patches of grass amid scattered mulberry trees spread around the stacked stones. The well stood wrapped in the shadow of a huge sycamore tree. And under the sycamore, a girl in an orange headscarf sat on the ledge of the well, trying to connect a bucket to the hook.

A thin ray of light peeked through the shade and expanded as it reached her and rested on her shoulders. She was young, maybe in her mid teens. Short and skinny and dark-eyed. Her lips were thick, open just slightly, revealing the gap between her front teeth, too white for her tanned skin. But her face, round and still and calm and lit like the moon.

He approached the girl with his bucket, watching her lower the pulley, slowly. She had time. She looked down into the well as the bucket descended. Morqos heard the tin hit the water and watched the woman wriggle the rope.

She stared into the well and swung the rope from side to side. Morqos stared into the shimmering black water. He watched the girl's bucket move from end to end, stone to stone. It wouldn't overturn. He looked up at her. The girl needed help – he needed to speak. Otherwise he'd never get back to the cornfields.

"You have to catch the edge of the bucket on the tip of a stone or something," Morqos said. "Or it won't feed into the water."

The girl looked over at the little boy as if she'd just noticed him, a knot of skin between her furrowed brows, thin and rounded like waning crescents.

"Have you done this before little boy?" she asked with a quiet condescension.

"I learned from mama," Morqos said. "I used to put a rock in the bucket but that only made it harder to tip. I couldn't lift one heavy enough to make it sink. Then mama told me to use the stone's edges. It works."

The girl looked down into the water, licked her lips, and relaxed her brow. The knot of skin disappeared into her forehead. She nodded and looked back at Morqos and held the rope towards him.

"Show me," she said.

He grabbed the rope from her hands and guided the bucket towards a sharp rock. It caught against its edge and turned into the water. The bucket sank deeper and deeper as he twirled the rope. The boy smiled and handed it back to the girl.

She sighed and shook her head as she grabbed the rope from him. She turned the pulley to bring the bucket back up.

"I guess I look like an idiot to you now, huh?" she smirked at Morqos. He didn't answer. He knew she'd be angry if he told her the truth.

"You've got some sense boy," she said. "Mama taught you well."

Morqos thanked the girl and tried to pretend she didn't say that. He watched the girl draw her bucket from the hook at the end of the rope.

"Give me a drink," he said, reaching for the bucket in her hand. The woman laughed and set the bucket down beside her.

"I never seen you around here before," she said.

"I'm from Koshk," the boy said. "I'm Morqos, son of Mina, a

farmer from Koshk."

"Ahh, the name, the village," the woman said. "A Nazarene."

The boy nodded.

"So tell me," she said, leaning forward and smiling like she wanted to play. "Why would I give my water to a Nazarene?"

The boy stared into her dark eyes that undid her smile. She was a fraud, hiding something only she knew beneath her glow. Maybe she fooled herself into thinking she was happy, trying to swallow the fear in her eyes.

"What do you need a whole bucket for?" the boy asked.

"My family needs to drink," she said.

"Your husband?"

The girl held her forced smile and stared through the boy like she was examining the dirt behind him.

"I'm not married," she said. "Not yet."

Morqos believed her.

"Brothers and sisters and mother and father," she said. "That kind of thing."

"They must not drink that much then," he said.

"My brother will be back here in the early night to fetch more water. Just a couple of hours." She sighed and leaned towards the boy, resting her face on her palm.

"It only fills you up for a little while," she said. "You're always thirsty in the village."

"I guess it wouldn't be a big deal if I got a little sip then," he said.

The woman stared into the horizon. She shrugged her shoulders, defeated.

"I guess not," she said, and raised her open palm towards the bucket. "But just a sip."

Morqos nodded and grabbed the bucket from under her, cupped his hands and dipped them into the water. He drew his hands to his face and drank. The water went down cold and sweet and smooth, the finest drink of water the boy could remember.

He was happy that he didn't wait until he fetched his own. He thanked the girl and wiped his wet hands on his face and sighed. For a moment, he forgot about the drought. Maybe she did too.

"You're welcome," the girl said and smiled at the boy, a real smile this time. he sat for a moment, lost in the horizon. She felt like a giant to Morqos. There was something huge in her quiet stare. Something heavy that held her down to the cold stones under the sycamore tree. The shade was her hiding place.

The woman pushed herself off the side of the well and stood. She walked towards the boy who had her bucket at his feet. Morqos noticed the tiny bulge under her galabeya, sticking out just enough to exist. He wondered what she kept under her long dress.

"So you're from Koshk?" she asked.

"Yes."

"By the mountains?"

"By the mountains," he nodded.

"You ever watch the shadows of mountains, how they move with the hours?"

"I never really noticed how they move," Morqos said.

"Right before the sun sets, they look like men."

"The mountains?"

"Their shadows. They look like men. All in armour. They surround your village and sit real still, like they're waiting."

"Waiting for what?"

"I wish I knew." She looked too certain not to know.

The woman grabbed her bucket, balanced it atop her head, and waved goodbye.

"Salam," the boy said as she walked away. He watched her move quick in the light, then turned towards the well and hung his bucket around the hook. He stood at the well for too long.

His father was waiting. He fetched the water and brought it back to the cornfield. His father was pleased.

The two worked the fields for the rest of the day, collected their wages, and walked back to Koshk in the late afternoon.

"Baba," the boy said. "Be nice to mama today."

His father looked at the boy and put his sweaty palm on his shoulder as they walked.

"She's a good woman," his father said. "But she's broken right now. The only way she'll know that everything is okay is if I treat her exactly like I did before Halim was dropped. Then she'll know. Everything is fine. Everything is still the same."

Morqos didn't respond because he didn't understand. He thought of his father's words as they walked home.

His mother sat on the floor cutting okra. He took a seat across from her. She looked up.

"Habibi," she smiled, and looked back down, mouthing something with no sound to Jesus. The boy picked up a knife on the floor – his mother was waiting for him. He grabbed a piece of okra and cut it into pieces, his hands still heavy from the cornfields, and threw the pieces into a pot beside her.

"I think my hands got fatter today," Morqos said. "I saw them grow in front of me."

His mother grabbed one of his wrists and pulled it to her face. She examined the lifelines in his palm, the rosy patch of skin under his thumb, the blisters and patches under his fingers and lined behind his nails.

"They are fat," she smiled and let go of his palm. "Fat hands of a little angel boy."

Morqos laughed. He hadn't heard his mother say a nice thing to him since his brother was dropped. Maybe she forgot.

She didn't forget. Thin streams of blood flowed through the white of her eyes and into the dark brown of each iris. He wondered if she saw the world in shades of red.

She asked the boy to pass her the pot and told him she didn't need his help anymore. He begged her for permission to stay. His father told him to get up and stop doing woman work. Morqos' eyes moved back and forth between his mother and father. A dull thud led his scattered sight to the table that sat under the sun's light. His father had plopped a watermelon on the table and took out a knife.

"She'll be a while," his father said. "We can have some watermelon until she's done."

~~~

The boy made it a habit to fetch water every day. His father allowed it. He said it helped him work.

Every day, the boy hoped he'd see the girl at the well again, her small body wrapped in the shadow of the sycamore tree. But she never came. Maybe the skill he taught her was too effective. Why would she need to be at the well for too long when drawing water could be so easy? But still, she'd need to fetch water for her family. He wondered where she was when he didn't see her, and walked away from the well disappointed every time.

Morqos wasn't sure why he missed her. He only saw her that one time. He didn't know, but it was something in the weight of her dark eyes that drew him. She was weak. When he stood next to her, the boy became a man.

Still, he couldn't find her. He'd seen so many other people at the well though. So many girls of so many different ages and colours and dresses. Even Bedouins. But the one he cared about never came.

A few weeks had gone by and still no sign of her. He arrived at the well one day, and in the shadows he spotted the man who picked up his garbage every so often. He didn't know him well. He also didn't know what use the man had for his watermelon rinds and empty bean cans. But that man was the only person the boy knew from Abu-Sandal. He was glad to have seen him. Maybe he could help.

The man spotted him and nodded as the boy approached.

"Don't you usually come with mama?" the man asked.

"Not anymore," the boy said.

The man nodded.

"I see," he said. "So your brother's still dead then."

The boy's fists clenched, his dirty nails digging into his palms, hard enough to draw blood, though he couldn't feel the pain in that moment. He wasn't worth the garbage Morqos' father gave him. The boy looked at the man and breathed quietly. He couldn't ruin his chance. The boy let his fingers loose and approached the man.

The man drew the bucket from out of the water with the pulley. Morqos knew he needed to say something. He didn't want the man to leave before he got what he needed from him.

"What do you do with all our watermelon rinds?" the boy asked.

The man turned to look at him. "Compost," the man said.

"Oh," the boy said. He didn't know what compost was.

The man was almost done. He stood at the ledge of the well and reached for his full bucket. The boy became scared. He was never good with small talk. He needed to ask.

"Do you know a girl in your village," the boy started, "with an orange head scarf?"

"Are you stupid, boy?" the man asked. "There are a lot of girls in the village."

"She's young, fifteenish? Dark skin? Dark eyes? She's got a gap between her two front teeth."

The man laughed and shook his head no.

"Skinny girl," the boy said. "But she was getting a little fat. Or she was carrying something under her galabeya, I don't know."

The man peered over his shoulder at Morqos, standing in the sunlight. He nodded at the boy as if he knew now. He knew that girl. The man picked the tin bucket from off the hook and made his way towards the village.

"Do you know her or not?" the boy followed the man as he walked away.

"I might."

"What happened to her?" the boy asked.

"You know what you do with a girl that has too many friends?" the man asked.

"What?"

"The same thing you do to a dog with worms," he turned his head and smiled at the boy as he walked.

The boy's short, quick steps couldn't match the man's stride. He was a few feet away from him and the distance only grew. The boy jogged to keep up.

"What does that mean?" the boy asked.

"It means God's justice," the man said. "I'll see you on Tuesday."

The boy stopped. He hadn't yet fetched his own water yet, and this man's words had no meaning to him. What did the girl do to need God's justice? And what was God's justice in the first place? The boy left with more questions then he came with. And still, he missed her.

~~~

That night, the boy laid down on his roof under a linen sheet and a blanket of stars. He could hear his father yelling in his home below him. Morqos wished his father would stop so he could hear his own thoughts.

God was up there somewhere, looking down at him. He prayed that God would bring the girl back to him. She was gone for too long. Maybe her family wouldn't let her out anymore. It was possible someone saw her talking to Morqos on that day. Maybe the person told her parents Morqos wanted to marry her.

The boy wanted no such thing. He'd found a friend is all. He liked her for her weakness. He liked her because she was thirsty. She gave him water. She listened to him.

She knew she needed to get more water as long as she lived in the village, she told him. You're always thirsty in the village.

She probably wanted to leave, to live in a place where the water flowed from the east to the west. She wouldn't need a bucket, she could drink any time. He liked her because she was unsatisfied. She wanted more, and he could see it in the bulge in her stomach. Whatever made her fat, all that well water, only filled her for a time.

The yelling below him stopped. He heard the patter of footsteps on the ladder that led up to his roof. He watched his mother's head bob from side to side, as she climbed up the ladder. It was a cool night, almost cold. She looked tired and calm. She was always calm after an argument.

She took a seat next to the boy, spread the blanket over her, and laid herself down. She petted the boy, ran her fingers through his curls as she stared with him at the stars.

"I've been watching the two big stars in the middle of the sky there," the boy said, pointing. "They keep getting closer and closer. I think they're gonna hit. Once they touch, they'll break to pieces."

"I don't think stars are physical bodies," his mother said.

"What are they then?"

She thought for a moment.

"Holes," she said. "God puts a big black canopy between the sun and us at night. Those stars are just holes. The light from the sun is peeking through."

Morqos considered her words. If she was right, the stars he stared at all night weren't really moving. Maybe he was imagining things. Or maybe she was wrong. He tried to count the stars. They were too many. And there she was, the large moon among them.

"What do you do with a dog with worms?" the boy asked.

"Depends on how you want to kill it," his mother said.

"You have to kill it?" the boy whispered. He heard her words and he felt their truth. They surfaced above his skin and slowly, slowly worked their way into him. The boy tried to feel something else but all he felt was heavy.

"To kill a dog because he has worms," he said. "This is God's justice?"

She thought for a minute.

"No," she said. "God gives and God takes." Her voice quivered with her words. "Man has no right."

She wiped her face with the linen sheet and sighed. The night was quiet. Morqos heard his father snore below him.

"I think he's alright now," his mother said.

She kissed her boy and stepped off the roof and down the ladder. The boy laid there for so many hours staring at the sky, though it felt like a few minutes.

In time, both his parents fell asleep, and the gravity of truth gripped him. The blacks of the boy's eyes grew between the brown. He felt the darkness condense into something heavy, the sky above came closer to surround him. The weight of the pale moon herself pinned him to his roof by her glare. Her calm. She had nothing to lose.

Holding his hands to his face trying not to make a sound, he cried like a girl. And for the first time in months, it rained at night. Light rain, but rain nonetheless. His face was wet from the rain, he convinced himself – not from his tears.

The boy thought about the dead girl on the other side of the canopy as the water from heaven poured through the holes in the sky. At least she had water now. Water as far as the east is from the west. She could drink forever.

EPILOGUE

A changed man from his bloody past, the years Moses the Black spent under the spell of a knife haunted him. He was a tall, dense man. Dark eyes, dark hair and dark skin. He remembered the wide eyes of fear of each man as he died, the power that came with fear, and the women that came with power. His body still wanted the women, but the past works of his hands that cut, slashed and stole crippled him when the memories arose. He fought them with psalms and songs for so long but they were only quieted for a moment. He was imperfect, his past filled with bad works and the blood of many men. He feared judgement. He feared eternity.

Anba Isidore heard Moses' pain. He walked him to the roof in the early morning. They sat and talked into the dawn as the first rays of a new sun pierced the darkness.

"What do you see?" Anba Isidore asked.

"I see light. I see a hint of a new day."

"A hint. It does not come all at once. The new light of dawn takes time to conquer the darkness of night, just as the new man inside takes time to conquer the old."

ABOUT THE AUTHOR

Mina Athanassious is a Coptic Canadian writer who was born in al-Abbasiya, a Cairene neighbourhood in central Egypt, before his family emigrated to Toronto, Canada when he was a small child. Mina received his MFA in Creative Writing from Lesley University in Cambridge, Massachusetts and currently works as an Intervention Support Worker, assisting persons with mental and physical handicaps with their academic endeavors. On his spare time, Mina writes and hangs out with street folk.

www.MinaAthanassious.com